Controlled Burn
The Evolution

By S.E. Lewinski

FIRST PRINTING, February 2022.
Harry Markos, Director.

Paperback: ISBN 978-1-914926-74-7
eBook: ISBN 978-1-914926-75-4

Book design by: Ian Sharman

www.markosia.com

First Edition

Goodwill Charity for the Planet
www.playingforchange.org

Other Books by S.E. Lewinski:
Rise of Samantha: Theory of Baggage (2015)
Coastal Traffic (2016)
Wasser's Revolution (2016)
Lesions: Evil is Coming (2019)
Melt With You: Made in Mexico (2019)

Dedication:
This book is dedicated to those individuals who take risks in their lives to evolve beyond the bounds of the status quo and make a mark in the world for humanity.

"If you are going through hell, keep going." Winston Churchill

Table of Contents:

PROLOGUE

This book is aligned to a series of current and planned books called The Thinking Series. Books based on change, contemplation, and what you would do as the reader. In this story, the primary character faces the question of human de-evolution and how his decisions will influence the future. The scenario of this science fiction story is the earth's isolated microcosms in the galaxy as it consumes, breathes, procreates, and devours limited resources on this planet. When does the population become a burden to the earth, and when will the dominant species realize it will face its own demise?

Everyone is concerned with his or her own life, living well, surviving, and being part of something bigger than normal everyday occurrences. Are there people around us, standing in line at the checkout counter, pondering what they can do to support humankind survival? What sacrifice would each person on this planet make to ensure all of our survival versus just that of the individual? Who could make such a decision, and would they be brave enough to be the individual to create the change?

This book is a sequence of events that builds on a progression of thinking. In our lives, we face many personal challenges that are prefaced with the trials and tribulations of living. Taking a backseat and allowing a non-decision will many times lead to an accumulation of fatal consequences. The book and characters represent the parallel to a normal life most people live day to day versus the chaos that is increasing daily around the world (war, poverty, economic failure, natural disasters, greed, etc.).

Have fun and enjoy the ride. This book hopefully will bring you closer to what's in your soul today!

CHAPTER 1 ⍦ PIVOT POINT

I guess the time has come in my life to consider what value I have to this world versus the action I may take shortly. Whether I will live or die is a big question on my mind since that has always been the dilemma lingering inside me. After living such a simple life — teaching, shopping, movies, a casual girlfriend—now I find myself distant from all that. To think that in my hands rests the fate of the world and what I have to decide right now…or walk away from it all.

During the journey to this point, I've seen the good, the bad, and the downright ugly nature of humankind. Being a target to be hunted and eliminated is one thing, but to consider that in the big picture, everyone has his or her own agenda in the end. Mine, of course, is still under contemplation, but fate intervened to provide me a push to be here at this moment in time.

Looking out over these mountains, there is majesty in viewing the magnificent cliffs and listening to the howling wind providing a chorus of chaos in the background. The steps I sit on were created by an ancient race that brought to life a productive culture, built an amazing city, and achieved control of this wild place that is drenched with continual rain. This civilization came to an abrupt end that was beyond their means as they were plundered and dealt a deadly hand of foreign diseases that engulfed their lives.

I'm sure they thought that a sacrifice would bring pity on them from the gods and that all would be well. However, in the end, no matter what they did, the cloud of doom descended over them and ended their great civilization.

How humankind has grown up over all these eons is truly amazing when you think about it. In the blink of an eye, from living in caves to traveling into space and deep into the ocean depths. Not all sounds so simple now sitting here by myself waiting for my mind to say, do the right thing…but in reality it's the ethical dilemma of going down in history as a perpetrator of genocide. Then again, why should I care after being shot at, chased, and condemned to die? The future may already be decided, and it's either nature or me that will provide the same outcome. I can preserve, believe, or have the courage to do what must be accomplished — or walk away.

Please forgive me in the words of the only God I know, for in your eyes, I hope you have a good heart as I must do what no man should ever have to face in life....

CHAPTER 2 ⛦ WORLD TRAUMA

One month earlier in Moscow Idaho…

I should have been a math professor versus meandering my career to philosophy. The amount of time spent grading essays is killing my social life— not as if I have one. As a math professor, I could just peruse to see if the student got to the right answer and provide them partial credit if wrong. Setting boundaries on the number of words has restricted the freethinking student, but the reins are still challenged with many of the late night word hackers. I don't really like to put students in a box, but the number of hours grading, interpreting, and reviewing written philosophy papers is starting to drag on my patience. Is it all worth it?

Staring at the stack of papers, I know the students continue to whine about why they can't just submit them online. Forget it, and then I would have to drag out my laptop and provide my cursory thoughts with cold electronic comments. There just isn't a personal connection with a student without the written words from a real person—that, of course, being me. In addition, it's much easier to scan the paper contents to ensure everyone followed the paper layout requirements or an immediate 10% off. I could go easy on format, but discipline in philosophy was one of my pet peeves.

Enough idle thoughts, I need to get down to business on grading. The yearly mid-term topic titled "World Trauma and Ethics" always brings out the emotional sides of the students. I found a demarcation between strong ethical positions to "why in the hell should I care." Brings back memories of one student who thought world trauma had to do with when a grocery store stopped providing his favorite Ramen noodle brand. Of course, that one went straight into the F- bucket since the attitude was more on the self centered side than the value to humankind.

Okay, let's start with the standard Liam random paper shuffle and get down to work. Paper titled "Fukushima Nonsense"— very clever title for a bridge to an ethical position.

'What humans conceive in the framework of development many times ignores the essence and power of nature, and that can wreak havoc on the pursuit of technological progress.'

I like that— one quick punch line on the overconfidence of humans in the face of the power of nature.

'As the population spreads across the planet, consuming the world's resources, humankind doesn't plan for future generations but instead focuses on the immediate comforts of the self-indulged individual.'

Wow, that sounds almost Star Trek Spock quality in phraseology. All right, time to skip ahead; this is for sure typical Carol Peterson's line of thinking, a solid B+ student who can put together strings of words to satisfy my proverbial personality. In addition, she's good in class and always keeps the rest of the students upbeat.

Closing statement:

'Our only hope for this planet is a consideration of a world union of leadership that brings together foresight, responsibility, and direction to manage the masses and to not allow technology to manage us.'

Okay, fair statement, not that it hasn't been stated in this forum before, but good enough for a B+ with my respectful comments for a mental challenge. Though it sounds a bit like world socialism, I had better not push too far or place my only thoughts outside the context of the topic.

"Carol, very good paper, I like your link between ethical foresight and the need for leadership that pursues the same. Would suggest an alternative path in consideration of the current state of affairs where no one agrees on anything from country to country. What might be the options?"

There, that should tidy up her B+ and keep Carol on her toes to do more research on the next paper due in a couple of weeks. Time to hit the fridge and a beer if I'm going to make it through another paper of world gloom and student's litigation on humankind. Crud, last beer left. I should have stopped at the grocery store but was too lazy with the rain and mud outside.

In past years, I had a passion for providing each individual motivation notes to pursue their best in my class. But over the last several years, I quickly passed them by for the next semester of students. Here I am thirty-eight and already reaching burnout as a professor at the University of Idaho. However, I do enjoy the town of Moscow with its low cost of living, zero traffic, and great outdoor wilderness areas. This is the first small town I had ever lived in after growing up in the California Bay Area. I never have to worry about my friends coming out to visit, since they don't consider this in line with their idea of a road trip location. At least for such a small town there are several Starbucks at which to hang out on a Friday night. Okay, let's see where this next paper runs off to.

'Overpopulation and Locusts.' The premise is that as we improve crops, water supplies, and infrastructure, people breed more, populations increase, then entropy undermines.

Hmmm…interesting point. Maybe another sip of beer before I read on with this one. The ethical position is that wealthy nations feel the need to assist impoverished countries, but eventually famines and reduction of natural resources prevail, and masses of people find themselves dead. Whoa, a very strong statement and looking like an A is on the horizon. Reading on, the circular reasoning is that the ethical nature to assist the needy backfires as populations grow due to improvements in crop yield, healthcare, and other means to support the populations. As time progresses, a point is reached where any additional charity burdens correction. The charitable care of population growth defeats the expense and value to correct the initial effort of ethical care. Wow, striking a spark of thinking that detracts from my normal liberal minded student— very deep. Need to give this student a boost.

"James, you took on a tough ethical dilemma that would normally be recognized as counter to goodwill towards mankind, but you also presented the outcome of charity without a consideration of the end effect, which is nurture more, but the end results in additional growth of human populations — in turn, unintentional consequences."

I noted that not once in James' paper did he mention the word Locust except in the title. I liked this approach since in all due sincerity, anyone with knowledge of entomology would understand that locust infestations begin with eating more, breeding more, then swarm. Hmmm, that appears to be happening everywhere except my quiet town of Moscow, Idaho.

Next paper, "Burn the Forest Down." Great, a student on drugs that missed the entire point of this assignment. It happens all the time and they derail off into an endless rhetoric of confusion. Who is this—Helen Zubar? This woman must be a late bloomer since she's about ten years older than the average student in my class. Never contributes much, just sits in the back listening, and has this gaze when I'm lecturing as if she's reading my mind. For sure, a strange cookie, this girl.

Let's see what she's thinking. Her ethical position is that we shouldn't consider forest intervention, in order to enhance the planet. Humans need to increase the burning of forests to attain what went unburned for hundreds of years in this country. Great, a female pyro-maniac! Sure, next let's burn down the cities at the same time. I shouldn't be so cynical, but this is way off course for this paper. A few more paragraphs and then a D– is in the works for Helen.

'In the greater quest of forest burning, at some point in time, humankind will either save themselves with the release of nature to its natural course or be doomed. The clock is ticking, and a pivot point will be inadvertent and inevitable for everyone.'

Well, I had better not be so hasty with the grade; there may be some mental issues inside her head that I wouldn't want to trigger into hostility. Maybe just throttle back a bit and think this one through rather than flipping the pages too fast. Hell, this is a small town, and how difficult would it be to find Liam Abram on a Friday night. I've never been paranoid here, but it seems like every several months some college student strikes out at a teacher with no clear alibi as to why. I know my colleagues during casual conversations say, "Never give an F unless you want an appeal from the student board of complaints." Yep, that would be an endless battle not worth fighting. Maybe I should just have a face to face with Helen and give her another shot over the weekend. Yes, that would be easier, and then I could give her a grade letter reduction for a paper rework. She should be able to stomach that much better without feeling the need for retribution—I hope.

Hmmm…wonder if Helen Zubar shows up anywhere on the Internet. She doesn't appear to be a very social person, but it's worth checking out. Let's see, with the name of Zubar, she should be easy enough to find on Facebook. I'm sure kids called her Helen Zebra when she was a youngster to drive her crazy. Maybe it was just the last name that defined her path to the present. Nothing on Facebook… maybe LinkedIn has a tidbit of information. All right, now I'm getting somewhere. Zubar, hmmm… actually a real last name but no Helen to be found.

Last effort—a random Google search for Helen Zubar…10,300 hits, but nothing that looks like my Helen here in Moscow, Idaho. I have to get off this kick of finding out about her; she may be some super computer hacker covering all traces of her identity. I feel guilty, like a high school student tracking down the best-looking girl to see if we have anything in common. Best to let this one rest since I have 25 more papers to go, no beer, and it's already 9 p.m.

I'll just put a quick note in an email to her and let it go at that.

Hello Helen,

Not sure where the disconnect was with the assignment on "World Trauma," but the contents of your paper weren't aligned with the set objectives. I can offer you a rework of the paper over the weekend with the lowering of a single letter grade or no credit on this assignment. Please see me tomorrow morning, and I can review the assignment objectives with you, and we can go from there. My office hours are from 9:00–10:30 A.M.

Best Regards,

Professor Abram

All right, Helen, make my life easy and just redo the assignment and put an end to this confusion. Now off to the next paper of doom and gloom.

CHAPTER 3 Ψ CHAOS THINKING

"Hello, Professor Abram."

"Oh, hello, Helen. Please come in."

Wait, could this be the same Helen who sits idle in back of my class? I didn't expect her to dress up with hair combed back and makeup just for me. Then again, maybe I'm flattering myself, and she's not out to impress me to provide her leniency. I never expected her to be the dress up type of woman, and a little bit of cleavage is quite nice to round out her impressive figure.

"Thank you, Professor Abram. I'm here to discuss my paper," Helen said.

"Helen, yes, please sit down, I have your paper here to go over with you."

Gosh, I have to keep focused here. I'm not sure what is coming over me, but this girl has some hidden charisma that is overwhelming my thinking.

"Helen, let me first state that you have very good grammar, writing style, and creative expression. The primary issue is this paper is off course relative to the assigned topic."

"Well, I'm very open minded. Please convey what direction I should take," Helen said with a nice smile.

Either it's my imagination or this girl is mentally flirting with me. There is no way I'll ever take that kind of bait for a grade change. It's one thing to internalize the attraction to this girl, but logic and training says slow down cowboy — take this bait and I'm in for some deep disciplinary trouble.

"Helen, the primary objective is to consider the content of world trauma and the ethical dilemma of the correction, change, and impact it has on humankind. Your paper conveyed that we should intentionally burn down most of the forest to recover the intervention that humans have had as a result of prevention of forest fires."

"Sorry, Professor, maybe you can provide me with an example of what you're thinking?" asked Helen.

"Well, the concept isn't to induce trauma onto the world but to take what is already occurring and then build an ethical question around the subject for changing. For example, consider how the Chinese Carp has infiltrated the Great Lakes, and how ethical would it be to use, say, genetic manipulation, poison, or some other way to eliminate them?"

Crud, why did she have to shift her body on the seat to invade my personal space? I could now smell her lovely perfume, which is a mix of lilac and rose scents. Helen is a little too close, and her eyes are beaming discomfort into my brain.

"Professor Liam, oh, I'm sorry, I meant Professor Abram — I think I got it this time," she said with a slight giggle.

Now this girl was definitely playing me more than she was five minutes ago. I rather feel like her pawn on a chessboard at this moment. Did Helen have a plot in mind with this paper to draw me into her spider's web? I think she knew what this assignment was all about but positioned me to get some face time. I have to stop this—my ego is flattering me because of my attraction to her, and that is the worst-case scenario that could come out of this meeting.

"Dear, that's all right many students get off track in philosophy essays."

What the bloody hell…did I just say dear?

Helen briefly reached out and touched my hand. "Professor, did you know you're blushing?"

Yeah right, not only am I blushing but this girl, woman, female moved me in a direction in just seconds with that one touch. It was like a tingle that rippled up my spine and electrified me inside.

"Ah, well I don't mean to scoot you off, Helen, but I have class notes to catch up on. Hope you understand?" I said, thinking quickly with the need to get some distance between me and this girl. "Yes, Helen, just redraft a new paper and you can hand-in Monday afternoon. How does that sound?"

"That sounds great, Professor, and thanks again for helping me out. See you on Monday," Helen said as she turned and headed for the door then looked back with an awesome smile!

What just happened over the last few minutes made zero sense in my head. It was as if I had just been run over by an ambulance and just stood still. I wouldn't throw away my entire career over this girl and flush my tenure down the toilet. No way. There has to be something up with the girl—she is hiding something. Logic 101 tells me that!

CHAPTER 4 ⚡ MENTAL COMA

Tonight an outing with Caroline, and considering, I should have just called and cancelled. I could have used the excuse of papers to grade, or class prep would have done the trick. However, tonight was her special night since we had planned on meeting at the Bloom restaurant, which wasn't only her favorite place but also where we had our first dinner date almost a year ago. I guess Caroline, in her mind, is pushing for a partial commitment out of me, or maybe she is going to give me her lecture on why women need to feel secure with a stable guy.

Caroline is an eclectic person about five years older and not my normal relationship type. Her two kids didn't add to my personal desire at this point in my life. Both kids are messed up since Caroline conveys, "I'm your friend" versus taking leadership to discipline both of them. However, though they appear to be normal kids, I'm sure both will end up figuring out life on their own versus following in the footsteps of Caroline.

Caroline had been married to a doctor, but I think he was tired of her erratic behavior—always late, messy, and thinking that everything from the grocery store was going to kill her. Though she doesn't have much money, she has an attitude that remains married to a doctor, and her status quo in life is the same.

What can I say, Caroline uses me to pay for meals, movies, groceries, and festivals, and I in turn use her for casual companionship that is in short supply in this small town. The last girl prior to Caroline I dated was a relationship jumper, and whenever she felt some level of closeness coming on, she made a jump. Not sure what jump number in Moscow I counted for, but truthfully, I really didn't care.

Ahhh, there she is, late like usual, hair a mess, and under-aged attire.

"So good to see you, Liam. You look so nice tonight," Caroline complimented.

"Well thank you, I just felt like dressing up a bit for a night out in Moscow."

"Hey, let's head on in. I'm famished," said Caroline with a grin.

I still wonder how this girl managed not to put on too many pounds even though when out with me she showed no remorse on ordering more than enough food for her and me. Then again, she always would take the leftovers, including mine, when we left a restaurant. I thought it was a bit unbecoming for a date to help herself to my leftover food, but considering whom I'm with; I'll just let it go.

"Good evening. Table for two?" asked the hostess.

"Yes, just the two of us," interrupted Caroline.

I was going to say yes, but Caroline quickly moved past me, which was a bit on the brisk side.

"This way, please. I have a nice spot that should work out for you," said the hostess.

Caroline cuddled my arm, which was cozy. Normally when we met up, there was no hug or anything, so maybe she was feeling a bit guilty rushing me into the restaurant. I have to be patient with her and not get myself into a frenzy tonight. Caroline, rattled by a divorce, two bratty kids, and still living like a teenager, has to be treated with care to avoid any discourse.

"Here you go. The waiter will be out shortly," said the hostess.

"Thank you," I said politely.

"So, Liam, do you know what today is?" asked Caroline.

"Ahh…Friday the 13th?"

"No, silly boy, it's been one year since we met here for our first dinner date!" exclaimed Caroline.

"Wow, how time flies and that does sound about right," I said with a sigh.

"Yes, and I've a small present for you to mark the occasion," said Caroline.

Wait, this girl had never given me a present since I have known her. Her motto in life was to see how much I could spend on her. Though I didn't mind, it's somewhat nice to have a touch of reciprocation from her.

"Well that is very thoughtful of you," I said with a complimentary smile.

I looked over the small box wrapped in tidy white paper with a small red bow on the top. Gee, hope it isn't a marriage proposal because then it would get ugly very quickly. Just give it a little shake.

"Well, open it up!" said Caroline.

"Okay…"

As I unwrapped the little box, my mind started to drift to the prior day meeting up with Helen. I still remembered that small touch from her hand that sent shivers up my spine. That made me happier than wondering what was in this little box.

"Oh my, it's a paper origami fish!" I said.

"Yes, paper is the traditional gift for the first year of marriage, but I thought, why couldn't it be the same for dating?" said Caroline.

"Very clever, Caroline."

I wasn't sure what just transpired—was this baiting me for a marriage proposal or what? I did appreciate the small paper fish—that was somewhat cool. However, in all due sincerity, Caroline wasn't the kind of fish I was interested in long term. In my mind, the sea was too big to settle down with this girl, and no way did I want to be her doctor number two. I know she nailed the last guy with some serious child support and vents on him during phone conversations—I've overheard them. Not sure, I would really want that kind of treatment in my life on a regular basis.

"Thank you very much." As I reached over to give Caroline a small kiss, she turned her cheek.

"You think it's stupid, don't you?" said Caroline with a pout.

"No, seriously, I thought it was imaginative and very much you. Also, the little box you wrapped it in was very special."

"Excuse me; I'll be your waiter for tonight. How are you two doing tonight?" said a well-groomed young man.

"Oh, just fine," replied Caroline with a cold voice.

"Great, I'll be right back with a couple waters," said the waiter as he deposited the dinner menus.

"Liam, Liam…what's going on upstairs? You seem, well, but so distant tonight," asked Caroline.

"Sorry, I'm just out of it tonight. You know, class assignments and proofreading a few publications for my colleagues."

Gosh, Caroline noticing something is wrong with me is way out of the ordinary. Normally, it's all about her world, and mine is just a little piece of her reality. I really need to just toughen up and forget about Helen tonight. I know she had made a quick move on me, but maybe I'm just out of touch with decent women approaching me. The minute

Helen smiled at me I felt my head start spinning. She gazed into my soul and spoke words I had not heard before. Like…

"Liam, Liam…you drifted off again. What's going on?"

"Caroline, please forgive me. Why don't we order and enjoy the night together?"

"Okay, sounds good," said Caroline while snapping a quick flip of the menu.

A student just walked in, which didn't surprise me since this place wasn't too far from the campus. One thing about being a professor in a small town, one was always running into students everywhere— at the grocery store, while pumping gas, or at Starbucks. I would say some run-ins were okay, but others were, well, a bit embarrassing. Like one time at Poluse Mall when buying underwear at Macy's with two female students giggling while I was buying boxers.

"Well, I guess tonight I'll have the Alaska salmon—looks really tasty," stammered Caroline.

"That sounds great, Caroline. I'm going for the pasta salad tonight."

"How are you two getting along?" The waiter stepped into our conversation.

"Oh, just fine," said Caroline with an abrupt shortness.

"Are you ready to order?" I asked politely.

"Yes."

I let Caroline order first, which in my mind was the proper etiquette. She ordered a glass of wine without considering that maybe we could share a bottle together. Just have to let it go, not get uptight with her self-centered behavior. It's almost as if she always wanted the upper hand to prove she was better than the ex-wife of a doctor or my Ph.D. in philosophy. Seriously, she must have figured out by now that her chances with me or anyone else in this town were nil. In the furthest reaches of my patience, I couldn't tolerate such disrespect every day of my life from her.

"Liam, can I ask you a personal question?" asked Caroline.

"Sure, go ahead."

"Well, we have been seeing each other for a year now, and I need to consider what it's worth to you."

I knew this moment would come eventually. I felt Caroline wanted a ring, an upside to her bank account, and a place to call home with her two kids. I really shouldn't play this out any longer for the sake of the two of us. It just wasn't healthy. I needed to choose my words carefully and be truthful.

"Caroline, right now in my life, I'm not sure where I want to put down any roots. I know we have been together for a year, but I still don't really know you all that well."

"Okay, so how do we change that? How about a long trip together?" Caroline said with a glazed look.

Trip…let's see how would that go? Her two kids, two dogs, and Caroline attempting every five minutes to tell me I'm heading in the wrong direction. Just driving around town was stressful enough with her. Then again, she could be thinking of a plane trip, but that would involve eighty plus miles to Spokane—that wasn't on my bucket list with Caroline. Of course, let's go on a trip if it meant air travel would be all on my wallet. Just not worth it with her.

"Caroline, you know I really enjoy our time together, but we are good friends more than anything else."

"So you have no feelings for me?"

"Truthfully, I respect you and appreciate your company, but I don't see this as a long-term relationship," I said.

I could see Caroline squirm with those words. I knew that wasn't what she expected from me, but I had to be at peace with her. I could feel the anger building inside her, and gosh, I sure hoped she wouldn't make a scene, especially considering one of my students is nearby.

"Well, Liam, let me tell you how I feel," said Caroline.

"Okay, please go ahead."

"I think, in your mind, you think you're too good for me. You live in a fantasy world at the University, and the rest of us locals are beneath you!" exclaimed Caroline.

"Wait, wait…"

"No, you wait! I'm talking, and I'm not one of your students that you can lecture to."

Time for the philosophy debate training to take a back seat. When anger ensues, all logic, control, and common sense are out the window. My only hope was that she didn't explode on me here in the restaurant.

"I've been a with you for a year now, and I don't think you give a rat's ass about anyone except your stupid philosophy crap and looking intelligent in front of your students. You just have me like some local tramp to hang out with until someone better comes along!" stammered Caroline.

Oh my, Caroline now not only had my attention but also about everyone else, who were looking over our way, including my student. All I needed now was someone to start recording video on their cell phone and post it on the Internet. I had to get this girl to chill out before this got way out of control.

"Caroline, can you let me speak for a moment?"

"Sure, go ahead," she said with glaring eyes.

"First of all, let me apologize for tonight. I didn't know it would turn out this way, and maybe we can pick up on ordering a nice meal—how does that sound?"

"Liam, you just don't understand how cheap I feel inside. It's like you use me, and I just want to scream out that it sucks!"

"Caroline, I totally understand how you feel, and I'm sincerely and deeply sorry you feel that way," I said comfortingly as I reached out to touch her hand.

"Liam, I'm okay being with you tonight, but truthfully, it ends here."

Wow, in less than thirty minutes it's gone from a slightly cheery night with Caroline to I'm a rotten a-hole who is self-centered and needs to be beat.

Truthfully, it's time to be done with this rollercoaster relationship. I've hung in way too long considering I never found Caroline to be my type. She needs a man that will go to work, take on her ratty kids, mow the grass, and watch TV with her every evening. In all due sincerity, I'm not that person, nor am I inept enough to be in that situation.

"Caroline, I fully understand. Let's just enjoy the night and talk about something else."

"Fine, just don't bring up your normal blah-blah on students. I'm in no mood to hear that stuff tonight," exclaimed Caroline.

"Sure, not a problem."

Gosh, what a night this turned out to be. Nevertheless, maybe it was for the best since this relationship was, in my mind, only for companionship. I know Caroline needs a man, and I'm not the right fit or person to be filling those shoes. This isn't my destiny in life to settle down and watch the kids grow, the garage being the center of my life, and pulling weeds each weekend. That isn't what my DNA is cut out for.

CHAPTER 5 ☿ MISMATCH

"Hello, Professor," said Helen.

"Oh, Helen, how are you doing?"

"Just fine and I just wanted to drop off the paper I reworked over the weekend."

"Sure, come on in, and let's take a look."

"So what topic did you decide on this round?" I continued.

Gosh, I hope that didn't sound cynical or condescending. I know that my mind was still on the meeting with Helen several days ago and the forwardness she projected. However, for now, I needed to do my job and focus on being a professor.

"My title is 'Charity, Poverty, and Consequential Mismatch'," Helen said.

"Well, that sounds interesting. Why don't you take a seat and tell me your premise?" I asked.

"Well, my premise is that the human race has a propensity for kindness, which is commendable. But in return, they fail to consider the consequences of helping the impoverished on a much larger scale."

"I understand, please continue."

"I referenced an article by the Brooking Institute that shows that world poverty has dropped substantially from the period of 1981 to the present by a substantial margin. The effort in economic development, agriculture, and clean water has had an impact. However, the consequences of these inputs result in additional human population growth, more consumption, changes in the environment, and eventually accelerated depletions of natural resources. Then you have to consider that when this dramatic population expansion comes crashing down, the humans will experience a calamity of unimaginable trauma."

My mind was listening, but my eyes were transfixed on Helen. Her thinking was a complete diversion from the rest of the class that reflected not just on the observable world trauma but also on the strategic results of non-intervention.

"Tell me, Helen, based on your premise, what conclusion have you deduced?"

"Humanity needed to be saved from themselves. I really don't feel they have the skills, the courage, or the drive to make any constructive changes," Helen stated.

"That is a very strong statement, please elaborate," I asked with a feeling of hesitation.

"Consider that the world population is currently at plus seven billion, take or give a few million. At some point in time, consumption will outpace the natural resources of the planet and humans will face a monumental collapse due to the demand," said Helen.

"So what would you expect to happen in the long run?"

"Well, most of us sit very comfortably in developed nations and focus on our comforts of life, which in reality continue to consume this planet. When food becomes scarce, water rationing occurs, electricity is intermittent, the volume of people on this planet will implode the entire world economy, and humankind will devour itself!" exclaimed Helen.

"Helen, why do you use the grammatical term human versus us?"

"Oh, I'm sorry; I wrote the paper as an outsider looking in. I felt that would be better than seeing the world as others do," Helen said.

"As others do, what do you mean?" I asked.

"That everything will always get better and we have nothing to worry about," said Helen.

Worry about, Helen had a good point—nothing to worry about was the mantra of most people. That is sort of the way I felt about living the "Caroline" life that had passed before my eyes the other night. She was concerned only with her life, kids, comfort, and me paying for everything, and the rest of the world could come tumbling down. Whereas, here I had Helen sitting in front of me thinking beyond what I had anticipated from her first paper draft on burning down the forest—which really worried me since a pyromaniac could do a lot of damage here in Moscow, Idaho.

"Helen, I'm looking forward to reading your paper, and for sure the contents hit a high note on thinking through the assignment on world trauma."

"Thank you, Professor, and I appreciate you allowing me another go at the paper," said Helen as she got up.

"Well, part of being a professor is learning along with the students. I've got to keep an open mind on the directions that students meander down."

Helen got up, and I couldn't help noticing her strong body and well-toned muscles that were not characteristic of most women. If she is working out, it must be heavy-duty daily exercise because not only was she a very attractive woman but also well kept.

"Professor, I know this may sound presumptuous, and I hope you don't take this in the wrong way. Can I invite you out for a coffee tomorrow night?"

Oh my god, that isn't going to happen. No way—I need to back out of this one right now.

"I know you're a busy man, but can I be truthful with you?" asked Helen.

"Well, sure, go ahead."

"I really like your class and the mental challenges you provide to the students. But I've got some other philosophical thoughts that I would like to share with you because I trust you."

"Well, Helen, I'll take that as a compliment, and sure, I'll take you up on that coffee offer tomorrow."

What the flaming, freaking, frick did I just accept a student date!

"Wonderful! How does Café Artista on Main Street sound, say around 5:30ish?" asked Helen.

"Ahh…yes, that works for me."

I watched Helen walk out of my office, and she turned back and gave me a smile. I just accepted an invitation from a student. In my entire career, the book of integrity and ethics says don't ever consider it. However, out went all the rules as my mind and my critical thinking jumped straight into the fish tank. Frick, I must be nuts! I know Helen was much older than the rest of my students, but when I last checked, she was still one of my students.

Well, I have an hour prior to my next class. Might as well consider what makes this woman tick and read over her paper. First, quick format checks as part of my rubric to ensure my self-imposed rules are followed. Looks like the title page is proper, margins are in line, justification on, five space indent, and double spacing. Font Arial 11 for ease of reading looks correct, and four pages of text are spot on, except this small food stain on the last page that looks like South America—hmmm weird, for sure.

All right, let's see where her opening statement starts.

"The presence of humans on this planet has created a civilization of diversity, culture, religion, and economic global presence. But the reality of time and the consumption of natural resources, though not fully comprehended, will lead to the demise of civilization."

Between Helen's verbal and writing, this was the third time that she was speaking as if analyzing humans as subjects. Sort of like me speaking about my parents as those people, without any connection that we're in a family relationship.

"The essence of caring for fellow humans brings a state of emotional need between the haves and have nots such that the political balances between societal pressures are attempted to be rationalized by politicians. Charity organizations, volunteer groups, and philanthropists make it their passion to create well-being for those that need it most. But in reality, looking at the consequences, the preservation of such groups drives improvements in wealth, healthcare, and prosperity that expands population growth and imparts burdens on the global resources that sustain such world population."

Whoa, now this girl is starting to frighten me. She's slowly working her way into justifiable genocide, which is a subject I avoid in most of my topics. I can only think back on how such thinking took a perfectly intelligent country in WWII into the worst genocide of populations, resulting in millions of death camps that served as an atrocity for my people.

Helen's paper, in a strange way, connected to her previous burn down the forest paper that defined a position contrary to the logic of self-preservation. This girl was somewhat scary in her thinking and could turn into the student stalker showing up at my doorstep. Thinking forward, that would put me in a position of dealing with the University Board, a negative mark on my life no matter what Helen would counter with. I would be tossed out of my tenure at the university with a career of discontent.

I had one other student who came on to me about three years ago, and she was very aggressive in getting on my good side to work her way into my life. I decided to approach the university administration to take a preemptive strike, and of course it got ugly, with the young lady implying I came on to her, which was completely untrue. Nevertheless, her words set a stronger emotional content with the university board, and I ended up having to write her an apology and resolve to zero contact moving forward. Was this Helen another round of problems I had no need to bring down upon myself?

I really needed to think my way out of this one and get my mind off the emotional side.

CHAPTER 6 ⴲ ETHICAL STAGING

Ahhh…there is a parking spot I could grab without a local six-wheel monster truck taking up space for two automobiles. Living in Moscow has its tribulations, but it's one place for sure where my Mini-Cooper isn't the norm for most of the locals' form of transportation. I associate my car with more of the student lifestyle, providing me a low cost form of commuting.

I'm reeling with thoughts. I could just be a no show and deal with the wrath of Helen; would she strike out at me in a way I least expected or feel compelled to try even harder to entrap me? No wonder I'm still single. My head always thinks logically, black and white—do not deviate from the path of conformity. Where has this gotten me except in all due sincerity, a boring life and growing old alone as a professor?

I needed to just go with the flow, meet up with Helen, let her down gently, and be done with it. Work her out of this affection with me and get her off my radar screen. That's what I'll do, and then everything will be cheery and back to normal. Hell, maybe she would just drop out of my class, which would be even better for me.

There's the restaurant, and I'm just five minutes late, which sounds appropriate. My head is spinning on this one, and I just hope no other students are around to gaze upon my stupidity for showing up to meet Helen. I had only eaten at Café Artista once and was pleased with the comfortable couches and friendly settings provided by the owners. The paintings on the walls by local artists provided a touch of a mom and pop establishment.

There's Helen waving me down. I somehow knew she would pick the cozy sofa in the far corner away from the few patrons. Get me into a comfortable position for who knows what. Now thinking ahead, I can't give her a hug, no handshake—maybe just a quick pat on the shoulder would do.

"Hello, Liam. Hope you didn't have any problems parking?" Helen asked with a smile.

"No, all was fine. Found a spot just down the block."

Helen looked into my eyes, "Well, I'm glad you made it, and it's good to see you again!" Helen said with a cheery expression.

Wait it's not as if I missed her or as if we are dating. That line is something you tell someone in a relationship, not a teacher–student arrangement. Best to refrain from any comments to bait her emotional state.

"So, Helen, do you come here often?" I asked.

"No, never been here before, but spotted this place the other day and thought it would be a good place for the two of us to meet up."

I'm hearing Stalking 101 words—need to be very careful with this girl.

"Great, so what's good to order for a light snack and drinks?" I asked.

"Well, I noticed they had pumpkin lattes and thought to try that for something different."

"Hmmm…you know, that does sound good," I said.

Ahhh, there's the server. A quick drink order and dash out of this place would probably be a good idea. My eyes are attempting not to connect with Helen. Her dress is more than I need tonight, a bit on the revealing side for my taste, but it did bring out her femininity. All right, she looks great, which is the last thought I needed in my fricking head tonight.

"Hello, so how is the lovely couple doing tonight?" asked the waiter.

"Oh, we are not a couple, just friends," I said quickly to avert any pretenses from Helen's mind.

"Yes, just friends," filled in Helen with a smile and a wink.

"So what can I get for you tonight? We do have a couple of specials tonight," said the waiter.

"Well, we both would like a pumpkin latte, and also, can you bring a few chocolate biscotti?" said Helen in a confident, commanding voice.

"Will do. Be right up, madam."

With a smile, Helen looked at me, "My treat, Liam."

"Thank you, very kind of you."

"So where should we start?" Helen asked.

"Well, first, it's nice of you to invite me, and I hope you understand this is strictly a student–professor meeting," I said, looking deep into Helen's beautiful eyes.

"Liam, it's actually more than that. However, don't worry. I didn't invite you to seduce, proposition, or come on to you."

Whoa, that I didn't expect from Helen. Here she is topped out in a fantastic outfit, makeup looking great, and she tells me, slow down cowboy. Now I feel even dumber than when I was parking the car.

"Okay, Helen so what's on your mind?"

"Liam, you're single with no immediate family, logical, and smart, and I believe you have the right DNA that will allow you to survive what I'm going to share with you. Please don't say another word. Let me explain since there's not much time left."

Gosh, glad we met in a public space; this girl is getting creepy on me. I thought tonight that I would be in the driver's seat. However, now it's more like professor, shut up and listen!

"Liam, I gave you several subliminal suggestions in the papers I wrote. I also injected you with nanotechnology when I touched you the other day that may have triggered several emotional responses. Including an attraction to me, which appears to have worked."

"Hey, you two look cozy. Here are your lattes and biscotti," said the waiter.

"Is there anything else that I can get you?"

"Ahh, no, this will be fine, and thank you," I said.

The waiter smiled, leaving me with Helen, my mind swimming—what the flip was going on with this girl? The logical part of my mind was saying walk, but the other part of me said listen, there is something here that needs to be heard.

"Liam, what I'm about to tell you will be retained in your mind if you are able to help me; otherwise, when you walk out that door, It will be totally erased from your memory."

Both my eyebrows must have gone up, and I was sure Helen could sense my nervousness.

"Helen, you're going to have to be straight up with me because right now I'm completely wigged out on nanotechnology and mind erase."

"Liam, how old do you think I am?" asked Helen.

"Well, I would say around maybe 28—for sure older than most of my students."

"Liam, I'm on my fifth lifetime, approaching 500 years in Earth's timeframe."

I could feel goosebumps on my arms and back. I had either a complete lunatic in front of me or someone who had gone way beyond the borderline of reality.

"Liam, take a deep breath. I'm going to show you something that is genetically unique to my being.

You may have noticed but haven't observed closely enough. I want you to look at my eyes very closely."

As Helen leaned closer to me, I could smell a light perfume and observed her flawless skin and hair texture. With just inches between us, I looked into her eyes, and as I squinted, I could see little squares that for sure were like no eyes I had ever seen before!

"Liam, what do you see?"

"What the…Helen, you have little square pixels like nothing I've ever seen before."

"Liam, that is the only difference between you and me in appearance, besides our extraordinary age difference of course." Helen smiled.

Time for a long sip of the latte and crunch down the biscotti. I had a feeling the night wouldn't be ending in the next ten minutes—I hoped.

"Helen, who in the hell are you?"

"Liam, as noted, you have nanotechnology that is streaming through your blood to protect you from what I'm going to tell you. Are you ready? If not, just get up and walk out right now, and all will be forgotten."

"Helen, I don't know what you've done to me, although it feels invasive. Tell me," I said without any hesitation.

"Liam, I'm the third wave of my kind to visit your planet. I'll tell you more as time permits, but my four other companions may have been killed by several world governments. I may be the last of my kind left to finish the mission, and the probability of that occurring is zero without your help."

"Okay, so where do I fit into the game plan?" I said with complete confusion. What's going on!

"Liam, getting back to my term papers, you were troubled by my choice of topics."

"Well, in relation to the other students, both papers were well written but way out in left field."

"Liam, your world has at most 50 to 100 years of life left, and the burden of the population growth and resource depletions will restart the clock back to the Stone Age—or a human extinction event."

"Helen, how do you know all this?"

"Liam, I was sent here to do something to change that outcome. Part of a genetic program that started tens of thousands of years ago is hidden deep inside my DNA," said Helen.

"Helen, slow down. I'm having trouble absorbing what you're telling me."

"Liam, that is all I'm willing to tell you tonight. We need to end it here so you can go home and think over what I've told you. In 24 hours, you have my life in your hands. If you go to the authorities, I'm dead."

I could feel a trickle of sweat running down my back as if I had just been thrown out of a plane and the chute didn't open. My mind was completely out of control. My logic, training, teaching, and being a professor all were out the window.

"Helen, so what about nanotechnology, which is sort of freaking me out?"

"Well, at some point I've got to trust you. I've searched for the last year for the right person who

I could connect with to continue my mission and I hope it's you," Helen said with deep sincerity.

"Okay, so what do you need from me?"

"I would like your word of silence, and like I said, in 24 hours, we will meet again. But for now, I need a cursory are you in the game, as you would say?"

I looked at Helen…what…who was this person. I mean, if she was whom she told me—I'm dealing with someone maybe non-terrestrial to Earth. I have to be truthful with her and thinking what if this Nano stuff just killed me if I said no. My mind was saying no, but my heart was saying yes. This just didn't feel like a chance meeting.

"So if I say no, you mentioned my mind would be wiped of you. Is that true, or am I going to drop dead so that no trail remains behind on what you have told me?"

"Liam, only a professor like you would ask that question," smiled Helen. "Like I said, I think you know yourself, and I think I found you for a good reason."

For the first time, I reached out and held Helen's hands. They were very warm, and I felt like I had touched another being that was here for good reasons.

"Helen, yes I'll be back here in 24 hours, I promise," I said without hesitation.

Helen gently squeezed my hands with confidence, and as I looked from the corner of my eye, one of my former students walked in. I quickly let go of Helen's hands, but I knew it was too late…oops!

"Liam, I trust you, and my life and soul are with you," Helen said with a glow I hadn't noticed before.

CHAPTER 7 ⚕ DROPPING POINT

I know it's not a good idea to be eating so late, but it was a great way to break the tension after meeting up with Helen. Driving home and getting drive-thru food was the last thing I would usually want, but tonight a thoughtless meal and a couple of beers was all I could think of.

I felt somewhat stupid considering how in the crud I was going to back out of what I had told Helen. Sure, in the heat of the moment, it sounded like a great idea to dash off and help her out, but after pondering it for a few miles, I decided I would have to be fricking crazy. The best thing would be to show up tomorrow evening, tell her good luck, and be done with her. Seriously, did she just expect me to drop my cozy life as a professor after working my butt off for 10 years to get a PhD.? Then trek off on some adventure with her to save the flipping world? I'm not even brave enough to go camping by myself, fearing Big Foot would grab me.

Might as well see what is on the television—no need to think any more about what had transpired tonight. It all had to be conjured up, including those pixel eyes. Maybe she got some type of Halloween contact lenses and then created a story about being some alien from another world. I'm sure she and her friends were laughing their heads off as to what a dork I am. Then again, she could take this to another level and set up some other bizarre event, and I could end up on YouTube, the laughing stock of Moscow, Idaho. The video would go viral, and then, lucky me, I could be named bonehead professor of the year.

Let's see what's on the news tonight?

"Limited information is known about the bombing, but by all indications, it was planted by a subversive terrorist group."

Great, another bombing and senseless killing that's all we hear these days.

"The nuclear detonation is being estimated at 150 kilotons and has completely taken out the USA base at Diego Garcia. How the bomb got near the island is at this time unknown."

What the flip was going on this is nuts!

"The nuclear detonation is currently being reported and viewed from several surrounding islands. No one from the U.S. government is reporting how such a bomb delivery occurred—plane, boat;

missile is unknown at this time. From all reports, the expectation of survivors is zero based on the blast radius. Our sympathies go out to the families of the men and women stationed at the base."

I needed to do a quick Google. I know that Diego Garcia is somewhere in the Indian Ocean, but exactly where is a good question. Okay, let's see, whoa in the middle of nowhere! Far from even the coast of India and Madagascar. It will take some time for help to arrive at such a desolate place.

"Reporting live from LA is Walt Brewer. Walt, what can you report?" asked the newscaster.

"Jim, the news spread fast, and it's believed that the nuclear explosion has already triggered massive riots. At this time, the entire downtown district is under police and military intervention. Looting and massive groups of people are currently unstoppable as they move from business to business. In addition, grocery stores are being looted along with any other perishable merchandise," said Walt.

"Walt, have you ever seen anything like what is going on now?"

"No, and I can tell you, the news crew is currently on the 20th floor of a hotel that is being overrun. People are in mass hysteria and rampaging the streets here in Los Angeles."

Wow, this was maddening, and I sure wished I had taken down Helen's cell phone number to call her and get her thoughts on the matter. I know she mentioned humankind was on the verge of a chaotic moment, but I didn't expect it to happen tonight. After talking to Helen and then the nuclear event, it's as if an omen had transcended that I never considered could happen!

"Next we go to Joan Hunt in Houston, Texas, for a report. Joan, can you fill us in on the Houston situation?"

"Jim, we are stuck on I-45, and the traffic has come to a grinding halt. People are out of their cars and are wandering aimlessly. We have seen windows smashed and random strangers being picked off and beaten for no good reason. Right now we are holding tight in the news van, but being a public icon, we are preparing for the worst."

""Joan, we pray for your safety, and we will keep the lines open," said Jim.

"Oh my God, someone just broke the windshield." As gunshots are heard, the news feed goes dead.

"Sorry, folks, we have lost our live feed with our news crew in Houston."

This was unbelievable, and my first thought was why would someone detonate a nuclear device on a small island in the middle of the Indian Ocean. I'm sure they considered access to the area and expected an easy target. Maybe it's the social effect—they anticipated creating chaos in all the major cities here in the USA. People must be wondering if their city is next or whether their family would be obliterated. This was making me sick to my stomach, and in a strange way, I wished Helen were nearby. It was somewhat difficult to sit here alone and deal with this.

My guess was that before the night was out, martial law would be imposed across all the major U.S. cities. I know my mind was racing ahead of me, thinking maybe it wasn't terrorists but our own people that detonated the bomb in order to stir up the masses; perhaps they anticipated this effect so a government lock-down could occur. In that case, a form of military rule could be imposed without any question. Maybe the time of the conspiracy theory had come full circle, and it was time for reality to become more bizarre than fiction. I've heard the crackpots on radio shows, but maybe they were just a trigger created to feed the masses information to move emotions on what was happening today. Another question is, how does mass hysteria work? Does it take just a crowd reaction to initiate chaos, or does something seed the inner soul to do awful things?

"We have just heard that the National Guard has been activated after several people have reported multiple random shootings occurring. People are being asked to return to their homes, but all indications are that riots are spreading faster than they are being halted by the police," said the newscaster.

I've had enough of this—need to turn the television off and focus on dealing with Helen. Ahh, a text message. I wonder who would be texting me this time of night?

Liam, just heard from the dean, please be notified no classes tomorrow, Cindy

----

Well, that doesn't surprise me. There is no way the students or anyone could concentrate after living through tonight with the riots and the anguish going on over a nuclear explosion. Everyone has to be thinking that it could happen closer to home.

I remember when my grandfather was alive; he would always tell me we have to be prepared. He had a stock of food and supplies kept in the cellar. Since je lived in tornado alley, he would tell us kids, if the tornado heads our way, we have just minutes to get to safety. I rather felt sorry for him since most of the food went to waste, and he died before a tornado ever hit the town. For no reason at all, tonight rekindled my memories of growing up and visiting him.

I'm not sure what will come of all this, but the decision to meet with Helen tomorrow doesn't quite feel like a choice but destiny calling me.

What the crud—lights just went out!

CHAPTER 8 ⲯ GLOBAL POSITIONING

Last night was more than I had expected after picking up a quick bite and settling down for an evening meal. Classes had all been cancelled, and hopefully, everyone just needed a sanity break prior to resuming what may never be a normal life again.

From the news headlines this morning, it looked like riots sprung up as an epidemic across the country and migrated across many cities. Global insurgent groups were all claiming victory against the USA to gain points with their cohorts. Not sure, I would want to lay claim to an event that killed thousands of innocent people and in turn destroyed families. Somehow that just didn't meet the ethical equation of what I teach every day. The bottom line is no one has been identified as the source of the nuke, nor has any motive been found.

I sure hope Helen shows up tonight in spite of the world trauma. Somewhat ironic that my last assignment became a larger reality than I ever expected. Now that I'm over the initial shock, I need to focus back on Helen and get more information out of her head. My mind churned in so many different directions after meeting with her. I thought it would just be a quick greeting, let her down easy, and then split. Then again, stupid me, I thought Helen had an infatuation with me. Coming to my senses, that was ridiculous since I think it's I who had the infatuation, especially after hearing her out.

Not that I need to play the shining knight rescuing this woman as my life plays out this script. I'm a professor and should get my butt back in the classroom and just walk away. However, I know if I pursue that path, I'll regret every moment. My only choice is to meet with Helen.

Later that evening…

"Helen, over here," I waved.

Wow, Helen looked very nice tonight, or was this just my personal bias? Her long brown hair, heart-shaped face, and close-fitting dress made quite an impact.

"Liam, we need to regroup. I'll meet you at Ghormley Park by the horseshoe pits in 30 minutes," stammered Helen.

"Wait, I'm not sure where the horseshoe pits are."

"Find them," said Helen as she quickly exited.

Whoa, that was completely unexpected, but then again, this was Helen, not your normal woman you would meet at Starbucks. Whatever was bugging her appeared intense. She didn't hesitate to pop in and out in less than a minute to contact me and be gone. Was she being followed, or did she want to meet in the park and end my life in a horrible way? Gosh, what am I thinking? I just need to grow some courage and get to the park in 30 minutes. I had better leave now so I can find the horseshoe pits before it gets too dark.

Since the park is only five blocks away from Café Artista, I can bypass jumping in the car. It should just take me about 10 minutes; then I can scout around and determine what is going down. Maybe she has a few thugs that want to rough up a professor to release some tension. Considering what happened yesterday with the nuclear explosion followed by massive street riots that could be the catalyst for more violence.

Might as well leave the server a nice tip. Who knows, I may never be back here again. As I got up, I noticed a few suspicious-looking characters in the corner giving me a once over. They didn't look like your normal Moscow crowd but more like uptight big city thugs. Best I just avoid eye contact and get out of here. Rather than dash to the park, I need to see what I could do to avoid being trailed. Gee, this just felt creepy having to sneak around the city. Helen didn't appear to be a weapon of mass destruction nor a serial killer. However, strangely enough, no Internet trail on this girl could be found. I think a quick hunch behind the monster truck and then a few back streets should give me a little cover. Seriously, I make a lousy secret agent mucking around and attempting to be stealthy.

"Oh Hi, kid, don't mind me," I said with a look of surprise on my face.

Perfect, just when I least expected it, there was a kid watching me all this time. Well, not quite like the movies; I had better get my ass moving. One thing I can say about the small downtown area of Moscow is that it's pleasant. Looking around, the neighborhood was quaint but very well kept and peaceful. Looking over my shoulder, it didn't appear as if anyone was tracking me down.

There's the park, and I was a little ahead of the 30 minute rendezvous time, but I still needed to find the horseshoe pit. I didn't even know people still played horseshoes considering there is no reset button or touchscreen. It was good to see a few families out with their kids tumbling around on the grass and swing sets. I remember when I was young my mother would always take me to the park, but Dad would hang back to watch sports on television. I never could figure out why the TV was more important than time with me. Talk about a kid baby-sitter—television, cable, and satellite have become the adult soma to avoid the reality of time spent engaging with each other. I know deep down, I'm still emotional about not having him around as a kid. Maybe that is why we only talked during holidays and birthdays out of respect for each other.

Yes, the horseshoe pits finally. Looking around… where was Helen? At least there was a bench to sit on while I waited for her, and no one was nearby. Reading several text messages from the faculty at the university. It appeared that everyone was as rattled as I was.

"Liam, there you are," said Helen as she quickly walked up.

"Hi, Helen."

"Liam, let's walk, and I can share more with you on what is going down."

"Okay," I said, being led by Helen in haste.

I could detect unease with Helen as if something was on her mind. If there was a time to be paranoid, this was it since what she told me the other day rang true with the recent nuclear event. Question: is she involved in some way?

"Liam, I'll assume you're good with walking several miles?" asked Helen.

"Yes, not a problem," I said without hesitation. "Helen, what is going on?"

"Liam, I said I trust you, so it's time to start trusting me and start walking."

One thing about Helen, she was in top shape as I struggled to keep up with her. "Helen, are we leaving Moscow?" I asked.

"Yes, Liam, we are leaving Moscow, and I hope that sits well with you."

"Well, considering I packed light for this trip, it sounds good to me."

Okay, I had maybe 60 dollars in my wallet, a couple of credit cards, some spare change, and my sunglasses. I couldn't feel more naked if you asked me to be launched to the moon. This was nuts, and I felt like a dumb puppy right now following Helen. She was truly in command while I tagged along for the ride.

"Liam, just a couple more blocks and we can stop. I've got a staging area for us all set up."

"Like a spaceship or something?" I asked then felt stupid with the question.

Helen did not respond. Obviously, she agreed it was a stupid question that had no merit or was worth a response. It was getting dark already, which made our exodus more comfortable than being tagged for termination.

"Liam, we have to go around the back of this house, so just hop over the fence."

Wow, nice staging area—an abandoned home on the outskirts of Moscow. Most likely one of many homes in the rural outskirts that were abandoned in the housing meltdown. Can't say Helen has great taste in comfort, but at least we can take a break after that more than brisk walk.

As I hopped over the fence, I caught a nail on my pants and it raked my skin, which went unnoticed by Helen, who jumped the fence with ease. I noticed a lock on the gate that was rusty and thought it must be more than ten years since my last tetanus booster—not a good time to worry about lockjaw.

"Liam, it's going to be a bit dark inside, so just stay close to me," Helen said with a comforting voice.

"Okay," I said.

"Better yet, give me your hand," said Helen.

Reaching out to Helen was warming. As she held my hand, it felt as if my life was entrusted to her. Helen's hands were amazingly warm considering the cool weather outside. It was nice to have her take my safety into consideration as we shuffled into the ratty house.

"Liam, be careful. We are going down stairs, and please don't freak out on me. I'll turn on the light once the door is closed."

I had to be nuts…lights are off…in the middle of the abandoned house and being led by what I would call my former student. We moved down a few steps; then Helen shut the door behind us and flipped on a light switch. As my eyes adjusted, we continued down the stairs into a dilapidated basement that smelled of mildew.

"Liam, please don't draw any conclusions. This is where I've been living since the beginning of the semester," Helen said.

I was mortified thinking that Helen could tolerate these conditions. I viewed her limited selection of clothes hung on an assortment of plastic and metal hangers. A small double mattress was raised up on wood blocks with plywood as a platform. The room was musty with an odor of water seepage characteristic of an old basement.

"Liam, you can take a seat here, and let me light a few candles and extinguish the lights. I'm illegally tied into the electric line and don't want to draw any suspicion, so I limit my electrical current draw."

I noticed all the windows were covered over with cardboard and tape to keep the neighbors from looking in. This was getting stranger by the moment, and God, I hope Helen doesn't pull out a gun. It would be just too easy for her to kidnap me, and that would be the last the community would hear of me.

"Liam, I want you to catch your breath. I'm sure you have plenty of questions. I figured before we move on farther, I owe you some alone time with me," Helen said politely.

Alone time—well, sitting here in this damp basement, I wouldn't call this the ultimate alone time. Looking at Helen, there was a solemn look on her face. This wasn't a girl who grew up at Macy's and had a life focused on shopping malls and her BMW. Here was a deep person sitting with me who was projecting a mission that was unlike anything I could imagine.

"Helen, we have a lot to talk about," I said.

"Yes, we do, and before we start, do you want something to drink?" asked Helen.

"Sure, what do you have?"

"Well, I have bottled water and sugar-free Gatorade without ice," smirked Helen with a grin.

"Let's go with the Gatorade, you can never have enough electrolytes," I said with a smile.

"I bet you're wondering what I'm doing living in a dumpy basement."

"Yes, that thought did cross my mind several times," I said with contemplation.

"I'm living off the grid—no cell phone, home, address, or anything you would call convenience. I use the library mostly for Internet access and the computer lab to write up your homework. My life depends on it, and shortly, yours will also."

Well, might as well go with the flow to get the low-down on Helen. Considering the worst case, I could still bail out and head home from this location. As weird as Helen was, I found it attractive versus the many women I've met concerned essentially with ancillary items. It's not as if I'm sitting here with a criminal but maybe the hope for all humankind.

"Helen, I'm not sure what's on your full agenda, but at some point you have to tell me what the hell is going on and where it fits into the big picture. Also, any insight into the nuclear bomb that destroyed Diego Garcia military base would be nice?"

"Liam, first I have no connection with what happened at Diego Garcia, but in a roundabout way, I do," Helen said with a sigh.

"I would very much like to understand the roundabout part."

"First let me tell you a story about what part I play in this saga. In my DNA reside three genetic programs that include the Seeders, Producers, and Evolvers. I'm the last in the line, the Evolver."

"Okay then, let's start backwards with the Evolver part."

"Well, as an Evolver, along with my four colleagues, for the last 500 years we have been the movers to prepare the human population for evolution."

My eye was beginning to twitch as a sign of nervousness. Hearing this from Helen was truly chilling.

"Evolvers are chartered to grow the human population to increase the probability of mutations. These mutations are random but are selectively targeted for a special purpose."

"Wait, I'm not quite getting this?"

"Okay, think about when the human populations were tribal and living on the plains and savannah of the planet. They had very little chance of increasing the gene pool because, well… not too many breeding choices. Now, if you grow the population to a global size where you have travel, multiple cultures intermixing, and unlimited interactions you create more DNA mixing."

I was buying this so far, and it sounded very plausible. This girl had lifetimes of thinking that I could not compare to my limited experience…. better just be a good listener.

"I'm following you. Please continue," I said.

"Now, think how people meet these days in terms of men and women. These events are essentially random occurrences, and the value is that it adds to the additional entropy of DNA mixing. Think with me as the population grows, the probability of given genetic traits will increase and add to a mix of humans that stand out from the evolutionary baseline. That is what me and my four colleagues have been doing for the last 500 years."

"Helen, how exactly did you accomplish this with just five people?"

"Look around you, Liam. Plastics, technology, and computers were just the start of triggering events. We also had our hands on land reclaim, food production, water quality, and other aspects that enabled the human population to bloom at an exponential rate," Helen stated.

Now my hands were shaking slightly worse than my eye was twitching, and I'm sure Helen noticed my complete insecurity with this conversation.

"Liam, listen to my words. There is a plan for humankind and for a very good reason," Helen said as she held my trembling hands.

It was nice to have her hold my hand. The warmth wasn't just in her touch but also as if she reached right into my soul and mind to talk to me. I've never been touched by anyone that had this effect. I could feel my nerves calm down and my eye twitch start to relax.

"Helen, I need to know the why part," I said.

"Liam, with technology, improved food production, better health care, etc., the humans bred more, which is the natural consequential course. Remember, we spoke on the subject of whether third world charity really helps humans except to make life better and, in turn, humans breed more. It's that simple."

"True, Helen but…"

"The consequence is the human population grows and grows and grows to about where you're at today. Then something new happens: poverty, fighting for resources, more people thinking divergently over religions, politics, gender, etc. The entropy creates more chaos, but for my agenda, it also creates the genetic diversity to evolve the human race," said Helen.

"This sounds like a great lab rat experiment, but why?" I asked.

"Because, Liam, in the galactic process, civilizations must evolve and control their future or eventually self-destruct or, worse, spread out into the galaxy and become the scourge of death and destruction. When the galactic society viewed the potential of the human species, the Seeders stepped in and added additional code to your DNA. Then the Producers arrived and started growing the mental state of the humans in science, agriculture, religion, and other aspects. The final step is my mission as the Evolver."

Wow, there go all the theories of aliens, secret societies, conspiracy theories, etc. Just a small group of galactic beings coming down to earth to tweak the growth of the society into an evolved species that will bring value to the planet and the universe.

"Helen, I understand to some degree, but I have to ask the proverbial question. Are you not to some degree playing God to mankind in these actions?"

Helen looked at me with solemn sincerity. "Liam, order is not free, chaos is, and that includes death and destruction in every aspect if we leave the humans unchecked. I know this sounds painful to hear, but the pattern in other galactic societies is no different."

"So I guess you're telling me what we humans portrayed in Hollywood scripts is truly fiction, and we don't turn into our own saviors of evolution?"

"Liam, that answer is based on probability. At this point in time, the human race is quickly approaching an extinction point," said Helen.

"Extinction—what's that all about?" I asked.

"The wheels are turning faster in terms of warfare, government turmoil, resource depletion, and water shortages, and the breeding population is on the rise."

Ironically, my last student term paper topic fit well into this discussion with Helen — almost as if the assignment was a primer for this conversation.

"Liam, look at what occurred post the Diego island nuclear event. Instead of solemnity, there were riots, looting, and more deaths. The stock market plunged over 4000 points even though Diego Garcia has no economic connection. Liam, the world reacted in chaos, with an instinct of further destruction and mass hysteria."

Helen had some very good points, and in spite of not wanting to agree with her, I wasn't pleased with the post-blast events as a reaction from the masses.

"So, Helen, what is next for the human race?"

"Hope is what's next, and my job is to deliver the last part of the equation before I find myself dead from those groups hunting me down."

"Helen, so what part do I play in this grand scheme?"

"Liam, I need you to be my trump card if I don't make it."

Whew, that is a handful to absorb. If Helen does not make it, I'm to carry on the mission. The only mission I have executed in my life is receiving a Ph.D. and finding a job. Beyond that, most people would call me a status quo individual with not much to offer the world besides academic rhetoric.

"Helen, why me?"

"Because when I met you and touched you, my answer was given. You have the spirit to succeed, and if it comes down to me sacrificing my life so that you can complete the mission, I'll do that."

"Why can't we consider that both of us will survive this ordeal?"

"Liam, I can't answer that question at this time, and one day it will all make sense," said Helen with a kind smile.

"You have to remember, I'm just as human as you are but with a portion of my DNA code released in an evolved form—where humans will be some day. However, if all humans had my evolutionary form of DNA today, they would self-destruct at a faster rate than the current path," said Helen.

"Why?" I asked with contemplation.

"Because the additional abilities would be used in negative ways," Helen said without hesitation.

"So, Helen, what does this advanced DNA mean for me?"

"Let me explain to you what I have inside me. In essence, when I touch you, it is more than just a touch. I can reach into your emotions and trigger certain aspects."

What the flip! Now is Helen telling me she is a psychic or what? Gosh, will this ever stop?

"Do you want me to demonstrate with a small example?"

"Sure, I guess it's okay," I said with no idea of what to expect.

"I want you to think of something when you were a kid that you have vague memories of but wish to relive."

Hmm, that could cover a bunch of topics, but I know the memory of my mother was always something I wish there was more of since she died when I was only six years old.

"Helen, this is rather personal, but I was only six when my mother passed away and I have that thought on my mind," I said with a quiet expression.

Helen reached out to grab both my hands. Again, I could feel the warmth of her touch, but it was more than that. It was as if she had connected with me into my inner soul. Gosh, this feels so calming.

"Liam, close your eyes. I am going to connect with you and open up your memories, as you have never felt before. But it is important that you only focus on your mother, or your mind will, for lack of better words, be overwhelmed," said Helen.

"I'm going to reach inward into your mind and you will feel as if time stops," said Helen.

"Okay."

"Are you ready?"

"Yes."

"Close your eyes, put the image of your mother in your mind, and let's dream together."

"Liam, Liam, it's time to get up, sleepyhead. If you want to go to the park this morning, we need to head out shortly."

"Yeah, Mom, and can I take my bike?"

"Sure you can. Just have to let me carry it over to the park. Okay, little cricket let's get rolling!"

"Mom, why do you call me your little cricket?"

"Well, Liam, it's because I love you and I don't think there is a better son on the planet than you."

"You sure? Billy seems like a pretty great kid?"

"Well yes, but he is not going to do for the world what you will do."

"What do you mean, Mom?"

"You have something I can't explain, but my heart tells me that when the time comes, you will do something that changes the world!"

"Liam, Liam, can you hear me?" asked Helen.

"Yeah, yeah…whew, that was amazing like I was back in time with my mom."

"In your mind are all the memories of being with her, and I just gave you a push to those thoughts," said Helen.

"Helen, that was stunning, and I forgot completely of being an adult and was fully immersed in my childhood."

"Liam, I couldn't sense where you were or read your thoughts, but I did feel much love and caring for your mother."

"Yes, I was only six when I lost my mother, and somewhere inside me I still feel that loss. Helen, I don't have words of appreciation for what you just did. It was beyond being human."

"Liam, you just had a taste of evolution and things to come. You remove turmoil, hate, greed, anger, and aggression, and something wonderful happens in a species. That was just a small morsel," Helen said with a smile.

"Helen, I hope this is okay, but can I give you a hug of appreciation?"

"Yes, that would be nice."

As I reached out and held Helen, I didn't want to let go. This woman sitting with me in this abandoned house, with minimal accommodations, moldy smells, and candles, was the most amazing person I had ever experienced in my life.

"Liam, are you ready for the mission?" asked Helen with a smile.

"Yes, I'm with you 110%. Ready to roll!"

CHAPTER 9 ѱ INJECTION

What the frick…I can't seem to lose these guys. I can jump over buildings and swim faster than them, but they are always on my tail. I know if I turn around and confront them that will be no good for me. Luckily, I have an infinite amount of energy, but this chase has been going on for hours and at some point in time, it has to stop… "Liam, Liam, wake up," said Helen.

"Whoa…glad you woke me up."

"What were you dreaming about?"

"This will sound stupid, but I was being chased. I had these super powers and could jump over houses and stuff like that. Unfortunately, no matter what I did, these guys were glued to my tail, and I couldn't shake them."

"So why didn't you stop and confront them?" asked Helen.

"To be truthful, I didn't have the courage to do that."

"Not so good, my friend," said Helen with a questionable grin.

I could use another few hours of sleep since last night was a handful. After Helen did her super evolutionary mind thing on me, I was totally convinced she was someone special. There wasn't any more question of who she was. Actually, I felt a lot closer to her than I thought could be possible.

Helen isn't like any women I have met in the past, focused on their job, or when the next shopping trip to Spokane was. Helen now dresses modestly, and no makeup was needed to bring out her best features. It was almost as if she glowed from the inside and didn't need anything to hold back her overwhelming warmth. I like her is the bottom line and hope that doesn't overshadow things.

"Liam, I hope you're not too hungry."

"What did you have in mind?" I asked.

"This morning you have your choice between bagged bagels, energy bars, or a banana."

"How about we split all three and call it breakfast for two?" I said.

"Liam, that has sort of a romantic thought to it," said Helen with a cute smile.

I could believe either Helen had me on the hook, had manipulated my male DNA, or was truly interested in me. Then again, I wasn't sure how personal interest would entangle with this mission. In my mind, I needed to put my life insecurities aside and just live for the moment. I'm always worrying, or having logical detours when I should just consider I have this amazing person sitting in front of me.

"Okay, Liam, our breakfast with some warm Gatorade should be enough to get us rolling this morning."

"Helen, what exactly is the rolling part?"

"Liam, I have to be truthful with you. I would like to provide you just enough information along the way to protect you, and where our final destination lies."

"So what exactly does that mean?" I asked with a grin.

"Liam, not that I want everything to be secret with you, but I have to protect the final objective. There is no backup plan; it either works or doesn't."

My thinking with Helen was compartmentalizing. Ever since we had met, she provided me just enough information to keep me moving forward. Since she was utilizing more of her brain than I was, I must expect her to be ten steps ahead of me. I can say for one thing, Helen isn't condescending, which is comforting. If she was, I don't think we would be sitting here together.

"Hmmm…can I assume you have an allowance for a backup plan of some sort?" I asked.

"The problem is we have only the resources we find on earth, and time is running out, so during this final phase, we have limited choices. So let me tell you a little bit more."

Great, another morsel of information to piece the never-ending story of mystery and galactic society thinking.

"As we spoke, your world is reaching a pivot point of potential destruction. The nuclear bomb attack is more than what you conceive it to be. There are factions on the planet that would like to have power over the entire world. Not that one world government would be a bad thing, but what you would refer to as a fascist government would be."

"So could that occur?"

"I don't think it will go down that path. Instead, the probability indicators project that those with nuclear weapons will launch, and what is left will be a wasteland for humankind's continued evolution."

"So what other options do we have?"

"Well, unfortunately, less than ten percent of galactic civilizations, if left unchecked, make it beyond the self-destruction point. The other issue is if humankind makes it past destroying the planet and spreads its seeds out into the galaxy. That presents another set of circumstances."

"Like?"

"For one thing, destructive sentient beings have a tendency to spread in a manifest destiny manner, which then adds another layer of interspecies conflicts—essentially being a parasite from a developing civilization," sighed Helen.

"So we are like bugs, and you want to ensure we remain under control?" I asked.

Helen held my hand. "Liam, true evolved beings don't look down on other species climbing the ladder. However, we have to be responsible for everyone's existence. We were placed on this planet to give the humans a fighting chance of survival and a push on to the next evolutionary step."

I'm sure if any of this is making much sense to me that external beings from some galactic society are dabbling in germ control for the galaxy. Hell, I've only been provided a few days of exposure to this wave of thinking and a world turned upside down.

"Helen, I am sorry, but I don't get it."

"Liam, your race has less than a one percent chance of evolving if left unchecked. Your race isn't in any position to reach the stars. The next phase in human life on this planet is de-evolution. Your society is splintered; it consumes massive amounts of resources, contaminates the planet with radiation, and pollutes the air and water. There is no rosy end on this path!" My directive is to save your planet and your species, not to be the judge, jury, and hangman."

"Helen, this just sounds so unreal. I mean, a part of me would like to go back to watching endless series, enjoying take-out sushi, and hitting a few beers in the refrigerator."

"Well, that is probably what the majority of humans would do. But think of the situations when the financial institutes collapse and world governments with power face tensions, what always happens—a melt-down."

Helen had her points; humans never want to face the music. We would rather just turn on the television, and the rest of the world can go to hell. Party, drink our minds away with sports, and be oblivious and sedated. When asked to stand up to save ourselves, it would be why should I have to participate?

"Helen, what really happens if we don't complete your mission?"

"Liam, simply put, the probability is high that Earth will be some forgotten planet in the galaxy and slowly fade away into obscurity for tens of thousands of years, until the next sentient being on your planet rises to the occasion," Helen said softly.

"We are it. We either act now before the turn of events collapses the planet or we go hide under a rock to wait for the end to come," I said.

"Yes, that pretty well sums it up," said Helen.

"Helen, why me?"

"Because, philosophy professor, I know that in the end, I can count on you to make the logical decision. Most of your human race would look at self-preservation, but you'll view what is best for everyone rather than just consider your own existence."

"Well, that's a mouthful," I said, considering being given such a responsibility.

"I have studied you for several months…well, not quite like a lab rat," Helen laughed.

"Oh really. What? More like a wombat?"

"Yeah, Professor Wombat!" Helen laughed.

This was the first time Helen had ever expressed any signs of humor. Most of the time she was on high alert with a sense of caution just around the corner.

"And one more thing, Liam. Yes, I find you very attractive, and I'm not your normal game-playing Earth woman. I like you!"

"Seriously?"

"Yes, without a doubt, I'm actually smiling inside telling you that and I really like being with you. How about a hug?" Helen asked.

"Yes," I said as I held Helen for probably way too long. Nevertheless, somehow, whatever happened next, I had to give this woman my heart and keep things rolling! I had never felt so alive. It was as if my entire life was in slow motion, just burning time on this planet, and then a huge slap hit me upside the head. It's not as if I needed to be sitting in some palatial restaurant or in a fancy house to be happy. Just being here with Helen was the most meaningful thing right now in my life beyond all the irrelevant stuff I had cherished prior.

"Liam, there are more things we need to talk about."

"Yes?"

"There is going to be a terrible plague I guess you would call it. This plague will sweep across the planet and has the potential to wipe out a large portion of the population," said Helen.

"Okay, so how do we inoculate or protect the populations?"

"Well, we don't since I'm not sure that can be done," Helen said with a sigh.

"Wait. Are you playing a part in this event?"

"Liam, the entire world is part of this event, not just you or me."

"So where is this going?"

"I have a genetically-modified flu vaccine that I can provide for the coming plague. It may not protect you, and I can't tell you if you will live or die."

Rats, the last thing on my mind right now is an injection. The sight of needles is one of my personal weaknesses. I can walk across burning coals or hang off a thousand-foot cliff, but I draw the line at needles.

"Liam, I don't want you to be afraid. I can sense your concern, but trust me, I have no thought of ever bringing harm to you," said Helen politely.

"So how will I tell if I'm immune to this plague?"

"My expectation is that you will only have a rash or hives if you are susceptible to this disease."

"Well, that doesn't sound too bad, so I guess it should be all right."

Last chance to back out on this mission. Somehow, I felt this was like a test of what would come next. I looked around me and could feel the damp room closing in around me. If Helen weren't the shining star in this dumpy basement, I would dash out of here right now.

"Please roll up your sleeve, and I will administer the shot," said Helen.

"Okay, here you go."

Helen slowly pushed up my sleeve and had no problem spotting a vein. Right now, my blood pressure is in full overdrive with adrenaline. Man, I just couldn't look. Helen must think I'm such a baby.

"There now, I bet that did not hurt one bit," said Helen as I felt a woozy feeling coming over me.

"Helen, I am really getting dizzy…what's happening?"

Blackness is all I remember as I fell into Helen's arms.

CHAPTER 10 ⛎ NOT IN IDAHO

"Liam, Liam…can you hear me?"

"Yeah…"

As I sat up, I could see we weren't in the basement where I had last found myself. This place looked rather sparse and was decorated like a one star hotel in the badlands of Texas. Well, at least I was alive, although I was feeling sick to my stomach.

"Liam, you are slowly coming back to awareness, so please be patient," said Helen.

Well, at least I couldn't say this was the mothership since the broken lampshade and dirty walls were not what I would expect of some higher species accommodations. I looked over at Helen, and—what the hell—it looked like she had aged twenty years and had streaks of gray in her hair.

"Helen, what the hell is going on?" I asked, looking down at my trembling hands.

"Liam, please calm down. I will tell you all that has transpired, but first we need to get you back to normal."

"Okay, at least a clue where the hell are we?" I asked with blurry vision, looking at Helen.

"Just south of Nogales in Mexico."

"Whoa, you have got to be kidding. It would have taken a few days to travel from Idaho to here," I said, stumbling over my words.

"Yes, it took a few days. I'm glad to see you are feeling much better," said Helen with a smile.

Helen offered me a bottle of water and a granola bar that I finished off in a few bites. I couldn't believe how hungry and thirsty I was.

"Okay, Helen, I need you to be straight up with me. What happened over the last few days?" I asked with a voice of contempt.

Actually, right about now I was feeling very pissed off over having been dragged thousands of miles without my consent. Then again, here is a girl that when I look at her my heart retracts. I may never meet such an amazing person again in my lifetime.

"Liam, I want you to draw on your inner strength for just a few minutes. I'm going to touch you, and hopefully, you will feel calm before I tell you another part of the story." As Helen reached out to me, she held my hand, and again I felt a warmth wash over me. I wasn't sure how this girl did it, but my heart rate and blood pressure must have returned to normal since my logical mind stopped and my emotions engaged, telling me to listen.

"Liam, I needed to get you across the border and closer to our destination. In addition, I needed to ensure that we weren't tracked or tagged while in transit. I considered a single traveler would have a better chance of making it here without any consequences."

"Okay next," I said with added contempt.

"Liam, I will be up front with you. I drugged you."

I could feel my blood pressure shooting up again, and at the same time, Helen squeezed my hand tighter to counter the effect.

"Okay next," I said.

"The part of the plague and your susceptibility was all for your emotional benefit," said Helen.

"Okay, and please explain the benefit part."

"Basically, you were easier to get in the trunk of the stolen car while unconscious," said Helen with an innocent smile.

Frick. I'm in Mexico with a highly intelligent criminal and now part of a mission with a woman I barely know. What in the world have I gotten myself into? My life was perfectly okay a few days ago. A lonely bachelor, sure, but content, safe, and not with a felon.

"Helen, are you crazy?" I said as I pulled my hands away.

"Liam, I would apologize, but how about a nice hug instead?"

"The hug can wait. Let's move on to the details," I said in a pissed off voice.

"One more thing—you now have gray hair and may look fifteen to twenty years older than a few days ago."

Slowly, I pulled the top of my hair down, eyed upward, and was shocked to see that my hair was gray. I stumbled off the bed and straight to the bathroom mirror. I stared at my face for several minutes and thought I was looking at my dad. I had wrinkles, sagging eyes, gray hair, and looked pretty screwed up.

"Liam, can I tell you something?" Helen said as she put her arms around me.

"What?" I stammered.

"This is temporary. It's called a disguise."

I turned around to look at Helen, and truthfully, she looked in about the same state as myself. However, this was still the woman who I had committed to make a journey with a few days ago.

"Liam I sort of like the gray version of you," Helen said with a chuckle.

"Oh yeah, but you kidnapped me and committed a felony by stealing a car."

"Yes, I know. However, don't worry about the car. I already sold it to a local Mexican guy to provide us some cash."

Helen holding me calmed my nerves. I knew that there was no going back to my professor life after being with this woman. This is like a movie unraveling with twists and turns that had way too many surprises along the way.

As I turned around to face Helen and before I could say another word—she reached up and kissed me on the lips. Time stopped as I was electrified by emotions I never knew were possible. My mind, my body, my thoughts could sense deep inside Helen's soul.

"Liam, how did that feel for you?" asked Helen.

"Wow, I don't think that was just a kiss!"

"No, it wasn't. You just got a glimpse of me that no other man on earth has ever felt. You're the first after living all these years that I decided to allow into my heart."

"Is this where I go blind?" I said with a humble and dazed voice.

"Of course not silly! Hopefully, you now have a better understanding of me and my intentions towards you are meaningful."

"Yes, I do. It was like I was lost in this euphoria, swirling around in a bliss of happiness!"

"I wanted you and only you to be touched with my heart. What you just experienced is the evolution that awaits humankind in the near future," smiled Helen.

Wow, I was blown away with the energy that entered my body. If this is evolution, there is no reason people should be looking elsewhere for happiness. I have never felt so positive and alive after such a brief encounter with evolution.

"So are you going to forgive me?" asked Helen.

I smiled back at Helen. "No," I answered with a grin.

"What? I thought we were past the first date," Helen said with a smile.

"Helen, your idea for a date with a border run is like nothing I have ever experienced."

Helen smiled back with sincerity.

"Okay, now that we look like mom and pop, how about we head out for a bite and see how our disguises work out," Helen said.

"It would be my pleasure, Helen. By the way, do you have a real last name?"

"I have taken many names in multiple places I have lived on Earth, but for now, let's just stick with Helen."

Wow, I am still mentally elsewhere after that kiss with Helen. She created more than an emotional feeling but a connection I didn't expect. It's as if we bonded in a way that I never expected. I think she just gave me a token of her love in a special way.

Taking a much-needed shower, Helen provided me with proper privacy as I cleaned up. Helen had procured some toiletries for me, including a toothbrush, comb, and razor. She appeared to always be thinking. I wondered if she even sleeps. Truthfully, it doesn't really matter. I am the luckiest man on this planet to be with Helen right now. She had billions of men to pick from, and I have to consider that I'm here with her right now. I have to put aside my insecurities, past worries, and old girlfriends and cherish the time with Helen.

Hearing a knock on the door. "Liam, I have laid out some clothes for you."

"Thank you, Helen, be right out."

As I walked out the door, there was Helen outfitted in a rather dated dress, a mismatched belt, and low-heeled brown shoes. I wouldn't say your top end fashion outfit, but hopefully not picked off someone's clothesline.

"Liam, not to worry. The clothes were procured along the way at local thrift shops," said Helen.

"Helen, did you just read my mind?"

"No, just your raised eyebrows and the smirk on your face. I'm not far enough on the evolutionary ladder to read minds yet, only perceive. However, there are species that do have such skills."

"Really?"

"Yes, in the evolutionary ladder, being able to connect with other minds takes a level of respect, empathy, dignity, and wisdom."

"Helen, considering how it could be misused on this planet, I would say best to leave mind reading to Evolution 505," I laughed.

"Okay, Liam, your clothes. Remember, you are an older man, so you need to fit the part. As an option, if okay with you, I would call this your last shave."

"Good idea, Helen. A beard or stubble would for sure off-set any facial recognition software."

Helen modestly turned around while I dressed. When she said that she liked me, it was about who I am inside—not as a pro-athlete or some guy outfitted to sweep women off their feet. When she said, "I like you," she was saying I like the person inside this body…nice!

As we prepared to leave, I felt a bit awkward in this outfit, and combing my gray hair wasn't comfortable. I could only trust Helen that this was temporary. I still felt young, but on the outside for sure, at least 20 years had passed me by.

"Liam, I spotted a little place called Taquería Momos that should work for a quick bite."

"Sounds good to me, Helen. By the way, you mentioned south of Nogales. How far south are we talking?"

"We are in a little town called Magdalena, Mexico. It's very quaint, and my objective was to get us farther into the interior and away from the border."

"Helen, how exactly did we get past the Mexican border guards deeper into Mexico?" I asked.

"Money of course," said Helen with a quirky smile!

Now, I could imagine at Helen's age, she knows more about human nature than I ever learned as a professor. In addition, she probably knows every trick in the book on how to get what she needs.

"Helen, have you considered getting caught? What would happen to you for bribing a border guard?"

"Liam, as we spoke prior, we're in a race for your species' survival. Failure or being apprehended is the last thing on my mind. I focus on angles, strategies, and probabilities of error when I look at every future move," Helen stated in a commanding voice.

Walking along, Helen reached over and grabbed my arm, which was nice. I decided to drop any more questions since maybe relaxing a bit would be better than probing every word. In addition, right now I am famished.

"There's the restaurant!" said Helen.

It looked like a safe enough place, a bit on the rustic side, with quite a few touristy-type people. That should help us blend in with the crowd. If anyone were on the prowl for Helen, I would expect they would not anticipate her companion to be some old guy.

"Hola, señorita Bonita!"

"Hola, mi amigo, y como estas," said Helen in Spanish.

"Usted habla Español muy bueno," repeated the waiter.

"Si."

Helen never ceased to surprise me; I could imagine she learned Spanish last night while reading a dictionary.

"Permítanme ofrecer los dos de usted un asiento junto a la ventana," carried on the waiter.

"Muy bueno, gracias," said Helen.

Proceeding into the restaurant, I caught a few smiles from the younger crowd. I hoped there wasn't an old people's section we should be seated at. The waiter pulled out Helen's chair; she sat down and at the same time brushed his hand. I could tell instantly that he was touched by her since he provided a kind smile back.

"Yo vuelvo con algunas aguas, y aquí los menús," said the waiter.

"Gracias," I said with the one word I knew in Spanish.

"Well, Liam, what do you think?"

"Helen, you speak Spanish very well."

"Thank you, Liam. I lived 10 years in Barcelona and learned the language while in a nunnery."

"A what?"

"A nunnery, you know a Catholic religious order."

"Helen, pardon my surprise, but that was like the last thing I expected to hear from you tonight!"

Whew, I wanted to ask so many questions, but it just felt out of place right now. Here I was sitting with this unbelievable woman, and I needed to just remind myself to go with the flow.

"Liam, I have a suggestion."

"Sure, go ahead."

"How about we call this our first date and we start with a couple of margaritas?" smiled Helen.

"Well, you're my kind of girl—let's go for it. Just a quick question and I don't mean to be a sponge as a date, but I have no wallet," I said.

"Not to worry, Liam. Let's call this my treat." Helen grinned with a sincere smile.

The waiter returned, and Helen ordered for both of us, including two margaritas and a couple of bean burritos with extra sauce on the side. She spoke fluent Spanish that flowed from her lips. My mind continued to ponder sitting here in front of this amazing woman. How could I ever size up to the vastness of this woman? No time to be insecure, since that has no value for my male ego.

"Liam, Liam…are you okay?"

"Yes, I was just pondering and thinking about you."

"And what in particular?"

"Well, are you like an alien morphed into a human being?" I asked while feeling a bit foolish opening up with a stupid question.

"Good question, Liam, and great place to start. I was actually born on a small farm near the city of Toulouse, as you could imagine, hundreds of years ago. I had a normal childhood until around my 17th birthday, when my parents planned to marry me to an older man from the adjacent town. I believe he was the town butcher or something like that."

This was not making a lot of sense. "So wait, you didn't land on some spaceship from the outer reaches of the galaxy?"

"Nope, born just a normal girl, with standard indoor plumbing," laughed Helen.

I laughed along with Helen since this girl has an exclamation mark on every statement.

"Amigos, aquí están sus margaritas y burritos. Me apresuré ya que ambos parecían hambrientos," said the waiter as he balanced plates and margaritas on a large tray.

"Muchas gracias," I said, looking over the meal with zeal.

"De nada," the waiter said with kindness, delivering our food.

As the waiter walked away, I could view Helen again in surveillance mode, scanning the room like a machine. It was as if she was memorizing every corner and nook to compare to the baseline in ten minutes. I had a feeling she was not only looking out for herself but also my well-being, which was rather comforting.

"Liam, what shall we toast to?"

"I would like to toast to meeting the most amazing women on the planet and for a safe and amazing journey before us!"

Helen toasted with me, and as we both took a sip of the margaritas, I caught a foamy mouth topping the glass. Helen reached over, wiped my lips, and gave me a small kiss that was amazing and nice.

Smiling back, I asked, "So, Helen, tell me a bit more about this 17th year."

"Well the 17th year was when my life changed. I was having dinner with my parents and sunk into a coma that lasted for several days. Of course, during the occurrence, there was no modern medical knowledge, so most of the town thought I was touched by the devil."

"Wow, so what happened?" I asked in shock.

"I survived several days of the coma, but during that time period was when the download occurred."

"Download?"

"Yes, downloading information of the galactic society transferred into me not only in body but in mind and soul. I learned about the entire master plan and my mission on your planet, including the Seeder, Producers, and my role as the Evolver."

"Wait, so how did you conjure all your evolutionary abilities?" I asked.

"Liam, I wish there was a good story behind that question, but I have no idea. During the coma, given strands of DNA were turned on and morphed into who I am today."

"No way!"

"Yes, all the conspiracy theories on aliens and other stuff aren't part of the equation. Earth in the galactic perspective is of low importance but positioned to be cared for," said Helen.

As I sipped the margarita at a faster rate and took a bite of the burrito, I found myself less interested in reality and more in Helen's life. I was expecting some type of super invasion by an alien species that would dominate humankind. Instead, this was sort of like a wireless mind transfer to bring Helen to our planet.

"Liam, I'm an evolver and the last of the series of the presence on your planet. The total of the Seeders, Providers, and Evolvers is just a few souls, with long lifetimes to influence human kind."

"But why?" I asked.

"First of all, it takes small pushes over a long period of time by a few people to create an end result. Our goal is to improve the probability of humankind's survival and evolution."

"You spoke prior on de-evolution, but what would happen if we move forward but missed the evolution part?" I asked.

"Liam, that is the reason why my life is dedicated to your species. As a society, your science is very close to understanding the universe and the laws that exist at the quantum atomic level. The human species, if left unabated, could launch out into the galaxy and unbalance the order that currently exists."

"Sorry, I'm not getting it," I said.

"Liam, let me be blunt with you. If your species launches into galactic space travel prior to evolution, then a higher intervention would be put in place to stop you."

"Are you serious?"

"Yes, it would be best for the galactic society and also the human race."

"Wow…I would consider civilizations out there taking time to evolve and would not want a pestilence race to filter into the neighborhood," I said.

"Liam, I know it sounds genocidal, but there are only rare instances of what I describe where intervention is needed. The probability right now for the human species is the de-evolution path, and they will never make it to the stars."

"Well, I guess that adds a little comfort for the well-being of the galactic society."

Absorbing all the information from Helen was somewhat overwhelming. Yes, she was straight up with me, and no matter how my ethical boundaries were approached, I could still view the logic in what she was saying. The human race is not the center of attention, and it could be a divisive element that torques the rest of the galaxy.

"Helen, are you lonely living here on this planet?" I asked.

"More than you can imagine. I may be the last of the Evolvers, and no matter how evolved you think I am, inside, my human side is struggling," Helen said with an expression of sadness.

I reached over to hold her hand and could feel her shaking as she spoke. It was good to view this side of Helen. She was just like the rest of us in many ways. "Helen, have you ever met the other Evolvers?"

"No, we were never to meet to maintain anonymity. However, inside my head, which I have trouble explaining, a part of each one was always with me. But for the past few years, I haven't been able to feel their energy."

I asked, "So are they dead?"

"I don't know, Liam. My sense is they are all dead, and not by natural causes. Probability tells me they were killed by external forces."

"You mean like other aliens or what?"

"No, humans."

"Why?"

"I wish that I could provide you an answer, but I can't!" said Helen with deep concern. "Each of us would die with the mission in our heads because it's that important."

"I assume you are not going to tell me about the end goal of the mission?" I asked.

"Liam, for your safety, I can't, and I hope you understand."

I already knew the answer to my question before it was asked. If Evolvers gave up their lives, and the human species is heading to de-evolution as a society, then the mission is paramount.

"Helen, for a kiss, would you consider telling me more about the mission?" I said with a smile.

"Well, maybe a kiss would at least get you to first base." Helen laughed, which was comforting.

This girl was for sure super amusing. We both finished our margaritas and burritos and called it a close for tonight. I could feel my old man's bedtime approaching quickly. Hmmm…one room.

"So, Helen, what are you thinking about sleeping arrangements?"

"Well, how about the pseudo human old gal gets the bed, and the old human man sleeps on the couch," she laughed.

I looked at Helen. "Tell you what. That fits well with what I am thinking."

I was here in this Mexican town of Magdalena with this amazing person who had me in her care. That is worth sleeping on any couch on any planet! Walking back to the hotel arm and arm, I was content with how things are unwinding!

CHAPTER 11 ⚯ BORDER ATTACK

"In the end, the world won't end, and life on this planet will continue...but maybe not with the current dominant species. However, some variation of in-breeding with another species will provide us with a better chance of not destroying ourselves."

"Liam, Liam...time to wake up," Helen whispered in my ear.

"Wow, thanks for waking me up. I was in a way too weird a dream about someone telling me what the destiny of the planet was heading towards."

"Oh really, and hopefully this person was pleasant?" Helen asked.

"Well she sort of looked like you," I said with a thoughtful expression.

"Oh really? Well, I hope she liked you."

"Not sure if she liked me, but she was cute."

Helen looked at me with a bit of malcontent, but not in a bad way. "We need to get rolling this morning for our next destination."

Hmmm next destination. I could use a couple of days here in this town. Though movie plots always say, keep on the move. Staying put is the worst scenario. "So where to?" I asked.

"We will be heading for a Baja coastal town and then will hopefully depart from there."

I figured best not to ask where we were departing from or how. I learned after talking with Helen that she would not reveal any more than what was needed to move forward. "Okay, sounds good to me and how about some food?"

I could sure use some food. I can only say that burrito last night didn't quite do the trick for nourishment after being out of it for a couple days in the trunk of a car. What I really needed was a good old junk food breakfast to get me moving again.

"Yes, we should pick up some food to store in our backpacks. That should help us to blend into the old tourist couple image," Helen said.

"Our best bet is to travel light and efficiently, so great idea," I said.

"Liam, one more thing."

"Yes?"

"I need you to start helping me with both your eyes and ears. I know this isn't your normal way of life, but wherever we go, scan, observe, look for the unusual, and don't hesitate to alert me," Helen said with a serious look.

Well, for sure, Helen was correct. My normal day-to-day life didn't include looking over my shoulder. The first time we came in contact, I could feel her looking right through me, as if she was looking for anything out of place.

"Liam, I can watch out for both of us, but with the two of us on guard, our chances of survival increase. Does that make sense?"

"Yes, I agree. I need to think just like you and be observant and suspicious of everyone," I said.

Helen looked at me with sincerity and said, "Please remember, we have to consider that the other Evolvers most likely are gone, and it's down to you and me."

I couldn't let Helen down. I had to consider if I were the weak link in this partnership, getting both of us in trouble wouldn't be good.

"Okay, we will practice, scan, observe, and report later. But for now, let's get some breakfast since I'm sure you are just as hungry as I am," Helen said.

"Helen, I hope this does not sound stupid."

"Go ahead."

"Right now I feel more alive than at any time in my life!" I exclaimed.

"Well, Liam, I'm glad you're by my side. I have always been alone in my life's journey. So if I trip up or say something stupid, please forgive me."

I smiled back and then gave Helen a gentle hug. It was difficult to believe that here I was in Mexico with an incredible woman who had swept me out of my reality. I could imagine not showing up for class was an alert for the department. They had probably already called the police and an investigation has started. I'm sure that's why Helen hustled us out of the country as fast as possible. The morphing of our age should keep us under the radar screen. I was quite confident Helen had the mission plan detailed out in her head.

"By the way, our next target is Guaymas, which is around four hours from here. The bus leaves at 8:00 A.M., so I suggest we gather our stuff and head straight for the station."

"Do you have the bus schedule?" I asked.

"I'm going on what the motel owner told me before you woke up, so hopefully it's accurate for us."

Looking around my predicament, I felt best to relinquish control to Helen. "Helen, you have full navigation command today. I'm still a bit out of it."

"Cool, Helen at the helm," she said with a wink.

It was nice to view the lighter side of Helen's personality, even under these trying times. She was a lightning bolt of energy, and that really added a charge to being here in this small Mexican town. We packed our meager belongings. Helen had bought me a set of shorts, sneakers, and a few other items, which filled the backpack. Both of us had running shoes that sort of didn't feel quite right with our age bracket but somehow should work for hitting the road.

"Liam, I already paid the motel, so we are ready to split. I'm just going to leave the key here in the room."

"Sounds good to me," I said.

The sun was still low in the sky this morning as we started on our way. The backpacks didn't add too much to our travel load. Helen shut the door, and a click from the latch catching could be heard. The window suddenly exploded in front of my face as I shielded my eyes....

Helen screamed, "Run!"

CHAPTER 12 ⲯ CITIES IN TURMOIL

The single bullet that struck the glass window was like nothing I had ever experienced before. Just a few inches to the left and my brain would have been blown out of my skull. I was still shaking from the trauma as Helen and I held our breath laying low in the alley behind some wooden crates. Helen appeared calm and continued to scan around looking for the all clear sign.

"You okay?" Helen said as she wiped my face lightly with tissue. I could feel the blood that was a consequence of the blast of glass as it shattered.

"Yes, I'm doing okay, but man was that close!"

"Well, I'm not sure, but I don't believe it's what you think it was," Helen said with a strange look on her face. I could see the wheels turning upstairs as she collected her thoughts.

"What do you mean?" I asked.

"Well, first, I don't think that was a normal bullet," Helen said.

"Oh really?"

"No. For one thing, I didn't hear the sound of gunfire, and with the impact, it was more like a sniper weapon," Helen iterated.

Was I missing something here? "Sniper weapon? What gives?"

"Well, it's a weapon that can be silenced and shot from long distances. I didn't hear a pop or anything, and that would be my suspicion," Helen said as a partial authority on the subject.

"Look, I don't know what all this really means, but am I to guess that most Mexican drug cartels don't have any of these weapons at their disposal?"

"No, most likely the bullet didn't come from the drug lord crowd," said Helen.

My head was spinning. I was thinking we would have a nice quiet breakfast, head out on a scenic bus ride, and have a great time heading for the coast. This was surely a wakeup call for me, the gullible city guy with no sense of personal danger.

"Liam, it's time to go. I don't think that the event was meant to kill us. Instead, it was a test to view how we would react."

"Like what?" I asked.

"Let's just get to the bus station, and then we can talk some more. Someone may be on our tail, so just put the incident out of your mind so we can focus on our immediate travel task," Helen said in a cold and business-like voice.

I have to give this girl some kudos for staying cool under pressure. I guess living for hundreds of years brings wisdom to potential dangers in life. Helen wasn't convinced that death was imminent, so I had best go with her instincts. Best we get to the bus station, settle down, and ride this one out for the next several hours.

As we walked to the bus station, Helen held my hand, which was comforting. I could feel the warmth of her mind and soul inside my head. It was early morning, and the streets were starting to come to life with vendors opening shops and people meandering the streets. This was really a very nice small town and I wouldn't mind coming back some day.

The difficult part of being here was witnessing the poverty so prevalent with broken down cars, ratty homes, and penniless people walking the streets. The one thing that most people forget is that most of the world lives this way. Struggling from day to day, these people have no safety net to catch them if they fall down on their face. Only hanging on with a few dollars, family, and friends to ensure life goes on—this makes me feel very sad inside.

Approaching the bus terminal, I detected no suspicious presence from anyone who may be watching us. "Helen, are you doing okay?" I asked.

"Yeah, let's just get our tickets, and then we can wait outside and talk."

That for sure was something we needed more of—talking. "Sounds good," I said with gratitude.

The ticket counter line was not too long considering it was early morning. I would guess many of the locals would buy their tickets to ensure a seat. I could detect cheap diesel permeating the terminal along with the smell of the food that was next on our agenda.

"Gracias a usted ya su bus sale a las 8:15 A.M.," said the ticket agent.

"Gracias," repeated Helen.

"Liam, why don't we get some food and sit at the little cabana outside. We have about 40 minutes before the bus departs," Helen said.

"Perfect food and drinks sounds great right now."

We settled on a few local breakfast burritos and grabbed several light snacks to carry in our backpacks. One never knows when the time will come for food, so best to be prepared. As for water, Helen weighed us down with as much as would fit in our backpacks, although I hoped that wasn't a sign of something down the road to worry about.

Sitting down for a change was nice as Helen and I settled down to the business of eating. "Liam, there are a few items we need to go over."

"Can you cycle back to the—what did you call it, a sniper weapon?" I asked.

I could view Helen's eyes darting around us to ensure who was listening, who may be watching, or possibly, if our disguises have been compromised.

"There are a couple things to consider. First, if my hunch is right, the weapon was used from a distance to avoid detection. Second, if they wanted us dead, we would have been taken care of by now."

Nothing like a burrito and intriguing talk. "Okay, so what options does that leave us?"

"Well, since there is a high possibility we have a tail on us, at some point in time, we will need to take drastic measures. Give me some time to ponder—it might not be for several days. My thoughts are that they want us to move to the final destination and then take us out."

"Okay, but why?"

"Well, for the same reason you're asking the question. It is what they will find—which I haven't told you."

"So do you think they know about or learned something from the other Evolvers?"

"No, they most likely have no idea. Evolvers would die with the information, and they fully understand the consequences. I think the other Evolvers must have evaded detection, but in the end, each of us is a key to one more cache of information."

"Torture option?"

"Torture may have been deployed on an Evolver, but they most likely took their own life versus relinquishing what we know," Helen said.

"So you would take your own life rather than confess what you know?" I asked.

"Yes, I know of five ways that would work even if captured or an imminent capture."

"Helen, I know you won't tell me, but are they after some kind of technology?"

"Liam, over the many hundreds of years as Evolvers, we have strategically pumped technology into your mainstream of science. Where humankind is today consists of small tweaks we provided that have led to your species experiencing explosive innovation and creativity."

"For example?" I asked.

"For example, in materials, we provided ideas, paths, etc., to create the foundations of plastics. Just a meeting or coffee with the right person is all it takes many times, and ideas become reality down the road," said Helen.

"Are you serious?"

"Yes, one doesn't have to sit in the lab and create polymer compounds but only plant a seed on how to do it."

"Wow, that's very interesting. So the five Evolvers do this seeding for hundreds of years, and before you know it, we have the atomic bomb," I exclaimed.

"Yes, even the atomic bomb is a consequence of technology implanting. There is always a percent of information that leads to warfare as an end to the seeds we plant," Helen said. "Think with me for a moment. The Seeders introduced the DNA to move your species up the evolutionary ladder. The Producers created the environment of agriculture, tools, society enclaves, etc. Then the Evolvers grew the world in technology and population. Each brings about small changes that provide direction and development."

"Yes, but that's all manipulation, is it not?" I asked.

"In one perspective, yes, but consider that the human race adds its flavor to the mix in the development. Your species adds color, creativity, and modifications, and that brings about uniqueness."

"But all this technology may also bring us to the brink of extinction?" I asked.

"Yes, you are one hundred percent correct, Liam. That is why you and I are on this mission," said Helen as she continued to scan around for any suspicious listeners.

My head was no closer to the mission and plans that remained inside Helen's mind. Would the technology the Evolvers planted be used in some way to get this planet back on track? Whatever she had in mind, it had to be very important.

"Liam, one last thing."

"Yep," I said while finishing off the last bite of my breakfast burrito.

"I want to warn you that during this mission we may have to make some collateral sacrifices."

I looked at Helen with trepidation. "What exactly do you mean?"

Helen reached out to hold both my hands. "Liam, we may lose a few people along the way. I know this isn't pleasant, but our mission is so critical we have to consider that as a possibility."

"Wait, do you mean we have to kill people?" I exclaimed while letting go of Helen's hands.

"In a manner of speaking; I said lose people for a good reason. We have to build a path to our final destination, and there may be a point when we have to cover our tracks to make it happen."

"Why?"

"Liam, please understand that life is why I'm here for this planet. But in order to preserve it, there are things that must be done or all may be lost," Helen said calmly.

"I'm just not sure I can do such a thing."

"Those are decisions that can wait. I need to consider a scenario where we may have no choice in order to reach our final destination—and we should just leave it at that for now."

A bit of confusion was going on in my logic of what Helen had just told me. How in the hell could we consider taking other people's lives for the sake of the mission? This was absolutely the most insane thinking that I could have imagined coming out of Helen.

"Please sit down," Helen said as she again reached out to me. "Consider we may be the last hope to carry the mission to fruition. If the time comes when we have to cover our tracks, we will both need to do the right thing!" exclaimed Helen with a strong resolution in her voice.

"But killing people!" I said

"I'm sorry for you to bear this burden, but yes, we may have to lose people to clear our path."

I could hear noise and unrest coming from the terminal. Something was up for sure. Though I couldn't understand Spanish, in any language, there are universal signs of despair. Helen noted the same and motioned, "Liam, we need to go!"

As we walked into the terminal, throngs of people were huddled around an old-style television hanging from the wall. I could see the announcer bouncing back and forth between pictures of some catastrophe that was going on. Helen listens to absorbing the story with more than just intent but the consequence of occurrences.

"Helen, what the hell is going on?"

"Just a minute," Helen said as she picked up additional information. "Well it is quite sketchy at the moment, but it appears another nuclear device has gone off in a remote region of Kotelny Island in Sakha, Russia."

"What! You have got to be kidding me!" I exclaimed.

"No, Liam, by all indications, it's true."

"Where in the hell is this Kotelny Island?" I asked.

"Well, just like your USA Diego Garcia, most people wouldn't have heard of this location. Like I said, it's a remote location and from the newscast, it was military in nature."

My logic was starting to kick in; first strike a U.S. military base, and now the Russians get a strike. Something was churning—that didn't add up!

"Helen, can we step aside for a moment?" I asked.

"Sure, just please give me a moment; some new information is being broadcast." I could hear the announcer speaking in Spanish, indistinguishable to me, but I could see on the faces of the people the turmoil of the event. Another nuclear bomb has gone off on this planet, yet I'm sure people have no idea that two thousand nuclear tests have preceded this event. Then again, most people in this world are concerned only around their own daily welfare.

"We have to catch the bus, so let's just get rolling," Helen said as she touched my arm with a slight squeeze. This was her sign to not hesitate—time to roll.

As we moved toward the bus, there were solemn looks on many of the passengers' faces. All of them had surely heard the news of the latest atomic explosion and the chaos that was commencing across the planet in less than a week. The question is, what would this all lead to? Someone had to be pulling the strings and I bet Helen knew.

Helen and I had seats near the back of this outdated bus. The upholstery was not only worn but also smelled from the accumulation of sweat and dirt embedded in the seats. I hadn't been to any third world nations, so I guess this was a great introduction to the reality of how the majority of the world lives. It was nice to sit down next to Helen after we placed our bags on the overhead rack that were quickly filling up. Helen whispered in my ear, "Please, no words yet, let's wait until we are rolling and there is less opportunity to be overheard." I nodded my head in acknowledgement.

Once the bus was finished loading, the driver boarded and started the rattling diesel engine. It must have sputtered several times before turning over. We had plenty of diesel smell filling the bus's interior. I'm sure the quality of the diesel here in Mexico wasn't the greatest and was a constant source of pollution. As the bus rolled out of the station, I reached over to hold Helen's hand—personally, I was really messed up inside.

"Liam, we can talk quietly now. How are you doing?" Helen asked with a tone of empathy.

"Truthfully, can I be honest with you?"

"Sure," said Helen.

"I'm really screwed up emotionally and somewhat insecure about all that's going on," I said, feeling like a small kid.

"I understand. Anyone in similar circumstances would feel the same pressure and stress you're experiencing right now," said Helen with compassion. I could feel that Helen cared for me. It was as if I could read her mind that she was in this for a good reason, and my life was in her hands.

"Liam, what is happening around us is terrible. The world has witnessed two nuclear explosions in less than a week on two continents that could unleash a barrage more to destroy this planet."

"Yeah but for what and why? Helen, do you know what is going on?" I asked her, reaching out for some clear information without the hidden secrets.

"Liam, I will be honest with you. I'm not privy to any information of what is going on in the world right now. Nor are these occurrences associated with my kind," Helen said.

"Yes, but why in the world would someone want to do this?" I asked.

Helen, with her analyzing mind, spoke, "Let's look at the several possibilities: USA nuked Diego Garcia then the Russian island; Russia nuked Diego Garcia then their own island; third party nuked both Diego Garcia and Russian island."

"Okay, but you missed one other option: Russia nuked Diego Garcia, and the U.S. retaliated by nuking their island," I said.

"Well, your philosophical logic is correct. I left that scenario out intentionally, including the scenario that both countries just agreed to nuke their own property, which is also possible. I have mixed thoughts exactly to the motives in general," said Helen with a puzzled look on her face.

Facing the various options with no motives was bizarre for each of the nuclear explosions. In addition, both events occurred in relativity-isolated locations.

"I know there isn't a good answer to the perpetrators of these events, but I'm looking at an alternate scenario," Helen said.

"What might that be?"

"Disruption of global society has commenced, and cities and people are in turmoil around the planet," said Helen with a look of concern on her face.

"What do you mean?" I asked.

"The pivot point has been reached, and we don't have much time. Remember, we spoke on an extinction path that the human species could meander down," said Helen.

"Yes, sort of," I said, attempting to remember the many threads of discussions exchanged with Helen.

"Without intervention the paths that result from these events could topple the world. When entropy increases, so does chaos," said Helen.

"What, are we going to unleash the rest of the nukes or something?" I said with contemplation of the worst-case scenario.

"Liam, please listen carefully." Helen spoke with a new conviction of seriousness. "We don't have much time left on our side. Most likely we are being tracked and maybe by individuals beyond the bounds of governments. Someone who understands exploding a few nukes in sequence would topple the stock market, financial centers, and governments and bring down the entire society. The damage will be self-perpetuating; food stocks will be depleted as people panic, riots, and the government power structures will all be in turmoil," said Helen with the wisdom of someone who has lived for centuries.

"Helen, are you scared?"

"Yes!" Helen said in a whisper.

CHAPTER 13 ⚕ DOWN THE COAST

The bus ride overall was rather solemn as I looked down the aisles. Most people, though many were sleeping, were most likely impacted by the world events churning through their minds. No matter how far away Diego Garcia or the Kotelny Island in Russia were, the effect they were having on the world was staggering. The last nuke rocked the USA, and I could imagine things only got worse since I left. There could be some presence of martial law and restrictions on travel disturbing the masses. Interstate commerce trucking, food production, and the so-called normal could quickly come to a halt. I know life is more rural and not as sophisticated here in Mexico, but I could feel discontent sitting here on the bus. Both Helen and I needed to be much more cognizant of harm that may come our way.

It's nice to have Helen's head resting on my shoulder as we roll down the road to Baja. I know in her mind she is carrying a burden that remains her secret—but for a very good reason. When she whispered to me telling me she was scared, I could feel a new reality to the mission. I think the odds just swung in the direction of urgency. My logic tells me something bad is coming. I could view a path of global war, with democratic governments turning into dictatorships overnight and, worst-case scenario, all the nukes being released. The world could be reset back to the Stone Age. Helen must have sensed the possibilities, and now her life was more than just about existence but a complex set of events that would influence the fate of this planet. I shouldn't let my mind race around like this.

"Whoa, how long was I out?" said Helen as she unsettled her head from my shoulder.

I looked at Helen and smiled. "About an hour."

"Not so good. We need to rethink our position due to the latest set of events," Helen said, and I could see her facial features take on a sense of urgent planning. This girl just snapping out of a slumber and ready to strategize was amazing.

"What do you have on your mind?" I said.

"Our clock just got reset in a direction I thought wouldn't occur so rapidly."

"What do you mean?" I asked.

"Well, first, if someone is on our tail and the world is close to a pivotal point of destruction, it shouldn't be happening so rapidly the collapse," Helen said in a troubled voice.

"So where does that bring us?" I asked, hoping for more information from Helen.

"We have to move faster and lose anyone following us very quickly. If world events move in the direction that I have contemplated, your species' extinction is imminent."

"What?" It's just Tuesday, and the world is nowhere near the end of its rope.

"When I state extinction, it is a path that will unravel over time for the human race. Once it starts, multiple factors play into the equation that lead to smaller and smaller pockets of survivors. I know this sounds improbable sitting here, but it takes much longer to build a global society than to topple it," Helen said with a seriousness I hadn't detected since being with her.

"I can fully appreciate what you are saying. I have watched plenty of documentary shows that demonstrate that society's interdependencies are precarious for our existence. I remember one show where in two weeks without food supplies, fuel, and infrastructure, people turned into barbarians."

"Yes, Liam, you are starting to view my thinking and a reflection of world events. I have no idea who is pulling the strings on the nukes, but at this point in time, it doesn't matter."

"Why?"

"Because once you light the fuse, it doesn't go out. Liam, intervention with the mission is the only possible way to save the human race."

I looked at Helen and reflected. My comfortable life was never going to be returned. It's not as if the mission is finished and I'd receive a ticker tape parade. Something was waiting in the background that I might not be able to fully comprehend the consequences.

"Helen, in spite of what you are telling me, I have this undeniable faith that the human race will work it out."

"I give credit to the human race, which has survived, innovated, and grown to the current state. Think with me, larger populations, political insecurity, weapons of mass destruction, tribal thinking, financial boundaries, and throw in religion and what do you have?" Helen asked with confidence that something would elicit out of my mouth.

"Well, then I guess you're stating the domino effect?" I said.

"Exactly, under given circumstances, one can control, manipulate, and move a certain set of events. At the current point, the human race is at a pinnacle where civilization is actually out of control. Thus, the fall will be monumental unless we take drastic action!" said Helen.

"What do you have in mind?" I asked, not really expecting an answer.

"Can't tell you quite yet," said Helen with a look of contemplation.

"Helen, I know you have a very good reason to keep some elements hidden, but it is killing me!"

"I understand, but I have to ask you to be strong since the entire human race right now—yes, right now—is in trouble and we are its last hope for survival," said Helen.

"Okay, enough of the deep stuff. What do you have in mind next?" I asked.

This trip with Helen was like attempting to piece together a murder mystery while at the same time, having the bad guys on your tail. However, I have yet to figure out who really are the bad guys. I know there was doubt in my mind about Helen's sincerity. She wasn't crazy or delusional about the trek we were on to God knows where. My mind was fully in the game, I had to let her lead, and when the time was right, we would have to work together to alter the path of the world.

Helen reached out to hold my hand. "Liam, I'm so glad you're here right next to me. Please stay strong!" I reached out and squeezed Helen's hand and with a small smile said, "I'm 100% with you and ready to roll."

As the miles rolled by, the remainder of the trip was relatively quiet except for several crying babies and the poor suspension creaking on the wounded road we traveled. The landscape, though bleak, had the beauty of solitude that was most likely the calm before the storm.

"Liam, before we go on any farther, there are a few things we need to clear up between us," said Helen.

"Okay, swing away."

"First, I would again like to apologize for tricking you and placing you in the trunk for the ride down to Mexico. Second, I don't have any special nanotechnology that was injected into you. That was just my scheme to get the needle in your arm. So can you please forgive me?"

Both my eyebrows went up on the disclosure from Helen. I had to give this girl some credit; she had courage that I didn't expect. For her, it was all about the end game and not looking backwards to achieve the end goal.

I responded with sincerity, "Helen, I know you were a nun for many years. How would you justify what you did?" I asked, turning the question around on her.

"Well…I guess, clever," Helen said with a smile and a shoulder shrug. This woman I had with me for sure was clever, smart, and amazing.

"I will give you that one! All isn't forgiven, but I sure am glad you pulled it off!" I laughed along with her.

I could view the bus stop up ahead, and it couldn't be any sooner. The seats on this bus had tens of thousands of miles of wear and left very little for comfort. Arriving in Guaymas, Mexico, was probably a good rest stop for this journey. Though the temperature felt like the upper 90s, the ocean breeze streaming through the windows lessened the impact of the hot weather. Living in Moscow, Idaho, the temperature rarely peaked above 85°F, which was great. Considering this was the farthest south I had ever been, I should be able to cope.

"Liam, let's plan on hustling off the bus, get our stuff, and mix with the crowds," Helen said as she scanned outside the window.

"Got it," I said.

I knew we had to be vigilant after the bullet incident in Magdalena and just about losing my head. We were easy enough to track on a bus, so I would guess we could still be on the radar with these guys. The key question is who and where are they? Do these people have any idea what Helen has in her head, and had they tortured and procured information from her comrades?

"Helen, let me help you with your bag. Just a minute…"

"Thanks, my shoulder is still torqued from the last thirty miles on the road."

As we headed down the steps of the bus, again I could see Helen scanning the area. Her mind most likely was calculating the multiple paths for an exit. It was comforting to be in a crowd of people, although just a few tourists could be spotted.

Helen grabbed my hand and said, "Let's head down that path over there towards the alley."

As I walked along, I couldn't hold back and asked Helen, "Why the alley?"

"Once we get down the alley, we will be able to see up and down, and expecting no one above us, we can move quickly. We need to then find a door to a business, home, or whatever and create a diversion path," whispered Helen.

I looked over at Helen with a flat smile; I got it for our next move. This girl had the wisdom of a wise owl, and I could tell this was not her first time covering her tracks. As we entered the alley, Helen started the process of turning door knobs or gently shaking a gate. We stopped in front of what appeared to be a little hole in the wall, and the door was open. Not that this was the safest alley in the world, but considering the consequences, best to keep rolling for the sake of the mission.

As we entered, eyes went up from what appeared to be the owner of this little hole in the wall restaurant. Helen, with her normal quick thinking, said, "Tomaremos dos burritos de chile rojo para llevar."

"Liam, let's sit over there in the corner, where we will be less conspicuous," instructed Helen. Thinking we were the only two non-locals, it was probably best to blend into the crowd with less suspicion. This place was quaint and typical of what one would expect for a little Mexican cantina. Only around 15 tables were scattered across the floor, with no two chairs appearing to be the same. The red floor tile was worn from the patrons and the years gone by. On the flip side, the food that wafted through this place smelled great, especially on an empty stomach.

I looked over to Helen sitting next to me, and she gave me that charming smile with the little turned up edge of her lips. She wore no makeup, and considering she was the quick, roll-out-of-bed type of girl, she looked great—maybe because I was looking into her soul, past her lovely green eyes, and short brown hair. I felt more alive with this girl than anyone I had ever met in my life. With Helen, it wasn't physical since the day she touched me and let me into her mind and soul. That was more important to me than any casual female kiss or a fling in bed. I felt my mind telling me this is what people need more of in order to bring them closer together—a soul connection with that other person that creates a strong mental connection. Not just two people that wander through life worried about the next generation of cell phones, how big of a home they have, or what they can whine about to keep themselves occupied. I'm not sure how long my time would be with Helen, but for now, this was the most significant emotional and fulfilling event of my life, and it made me feel alive!

"Are you doing okay over there?" Helen asked in a diminutive voice.

"Yeah, doing okay. Actually, I was just thinking about you."

"Oh yeah, and what is running through your mind?" Helen asked.

I looked at Helen and thought, should I tell her what is running through my head? Yes, be truthful and upfront. "Helen, I was just thinking what an amazing mental and emotional connection I have with you!"

With one raised eyebrow, Helen looked at me, pulling me closer to tell her more. "Keep going…"

"From my heart, this is the first time that my priority isn't physical, although you're great looking and attractive. My spirit, my libido is like zipped tight with you for lack of better words."

Helen immediately started laughing. "Zip up. Liam, you are truly a woman's best nerdy friend!"

I smiled back with my eyes rolling back and forth. "Thanks, I will take that as a compliment, but may I elaborate for the sake of the discussion?"

"Sure, carry on please."

"Well, it's like when you first came to my office you did catch my eye. However, being one of my students, it was hands off. Not to be disrespectful but you also looked a bit older than other students," I said.

"Oh yeah, student, but possibly a little older lady escapade," Helen said with a smile.

"Helen, I have to watch my words here. I was sort of contemplating meeting you in my mind."

"Oh yeah and did you have a plan?"

"Of course not. You jumped me on that one." I laughed as Helen smiled back.

"In the last several days, this roller coaster ride has been more lively than anything I have ever done in all my life. Finally yet importantly, I don't want to jump in bed with you as a woman for the first time in my life. Okay, there, I said it!"

Helen reached out to hold my hand. I could feel the serious talk coming my way. "Liam, when I let you touch my soul, we bonded more than any intimate experience could ever bring between the two of us."

"I know and I can feel it," I said.

"You have touched evolution, beyond just the physical. Just think of a world where everyone could exist in the same state, not worried about living in their personal shell but reaching out and touching other souls in a very deep way."

"Yes, things would be radically different," I said with a new sense of contemplation.

I was truly in a different world with Helen right now. I could imagine if I had spoken those words with any other girl she would probably walk out and tell all her friends I was some freak. The senseless games I had played meeting women, propping myself up on a stick to get their attention, truthfully wasn't that satisfying for me.

"Liam, you have touched what the future of earth could be like. Our mission is to increase the probability that humankind has a future, but seeded with evolution and not bent on self-destruction." Helen said.

"Helen, looks like our burritos are on the way, let's get out of here," I said, looking for an exit.

As we shuffled out the front of the little hole-in-the-wall restaurant, we found ourselves on the touristy side of this town with a mix of locals and foreigners. That allowed us to blend in with the crowd and distract any possible pursuers. I could detect Helen's internal radar scanning our next move.

"Helen, are we planning on staying here tonight?"

"No, we need to get to the harbor for our next connection," she said.

"Can you tell me where that may be?"

"Down the coast farther into South America is probably enough for now. We need to hurry," said Helen.

This was not the time to challenge Helen with additional questions. Considering the size of South America, this could be quite the leg on the journey, so I had best be patient. The crowd didn't appear to be thinning since this coastal town appeared popular with tourists. That was good for us to blend in, and I'm sure that was Helen's plan.

"Liam, we need to hit that grocery store down the street and load up with supplies. This may be our last chance to get the supplies that we need for the next several days."

"Okay, and what are you thinking we need?" I enquired, knowing this wouldn't be a camping trip.

"We both need to load up on water, high energy food, and granola bars, and it's probably best to pick up medical supplies," Helen said.

Looking at her, I said, "I'm not much of a world traveler, so how about you pick out what we need, and I will act as the donkey?"

"I think you meant burro for this particular region—either way, sounds like a good plan," smiled Helen.

As we entered the small grocery store with only about thirty assorted racks, Helen went to work with the basket picking out various items. She was thinking compact and high energy for sure, since she went straight for things like nuts and granola bars and avoided what I would typically categorize as junk food. I hoped that we would take a break soon to chow down on the burritos we picked up. Helen also found a few medicines scripted in Spanish, so I would suspect they were value added for headaches or pain. I would suspect we would need some basics like aspirin and something for a stomach bug we were bound to pick up.

"Liam, please pick up that box of wipes. That may come in handy and the white gauze and cotton pads. Not sure if we will need those, but it never hurts."

As we proceeded to the cash register, Helen pulled out Mexican pesos to pay and appeared to have enough for the cashier. However, she was careful not to allow the clerk to view what she really had in her wallet in terms of cash. Probably a great move considering where we were currently. We packed all our supplies in every nook we could find in our packs. Extra bottles of water went in outside pockets, and I slipped one in my pants as the last place.

"Liam, we have a little time, and I spotted a park bench just down the road under a tree. We need to have a tactical discussion on our next steps. Also, I really need to eat something before I pass out."

"Agreed. I'm famished and need an energy boost," I said.

We approached the location, and I spotted the crudely constructed bench cast out of concrete and red tiles for seat pads. Someone had put their creativity into this bench since it was not mainstream. The acacia tree was perfect, casting a nice shadow to relieve us of the overhead sun. Helen attended to our burritos and kindly unwrapped one for me, which was nice. She surely knew how to provide a small gesture of politeness and caring for me. In no time, we both consumed the burritos that were at least twice the size I was used to getting in the US.

"Liam, it's time for a serious talk."

"I'm all ears," I said, contemplating what would come next.

"Well, first I have a large selection of uncut diamonds with me."

"Okay...." Better not ask Helen how these came about.

"They are hidden in both our backpacks but can be easily removed. We have to take extra care since this is all we have to make it to our final destination. In addition, we can expect someone will attempt to steal them from us," Helen said.

"Around how much are we talking?" I asked.

"I would tell you, but it's not important right now, and—"

"—best to limit what I know," I interrupted while Helen was speaking.

"Yes, you're getting the hang of things, Liam," Helen said politely.

"Our next step on the mission is to catch a boat down the coast to South America. I made connections with a freighter several weeks ago, and it should be waiting for us for the outbound trip. Now here is what you need to be aware of. We will be paying the captain $200,000 in uncut diamonds with no questions asked," said Helen.

"What? $200K—you've got to be kidding me," I exclaimed. "Wouldn't it have been cheaper to fly?"

"Yes, it's cheaper to fly, but we would show up on someone's radar, which isn't what we need right now," said Helen.

I could contemplate Helen had ten steps always planned, including the latest one, especially considering I didn't normally have diamonds lying around to use for bartering portage on a freighter. Again, not worth asking where she got the diamonds, but maybe she'd tell me later.

"There is one more important point you need to be aware of. This freighter is a front for drug runners and, you could say, a questionable bunch of characters. They will only deal with a man, so you're going to make the exchange while I serve as your female translator and travel companion," said Helen.

"Helen, that's a lot to swallow. What's not to stop them from clobbering us and throwing us overboard?" I asked with deep concern.

"Well, in the drug world, anyone that uses diamonds normally means trouble if you mess with them. You represent an unknown to them, backed by high value, and that's all they need to know," said Helen.

Right now, I needed to just consider Helen was running the show and follow her lead rather than get emotional about what was about to go down.

"What else should I consider?"

"When we meet up with the boat captain, no small talk. Just state your name is Taylor, and hand him the bag of diamonds. I will translate in Spanish, but don't say anything else in English because we don't know if anyone can understand."

"Okay, sounds reasonable. When do we meet up with the boat?" I asked.

"We have about an hour to make it down to the dock. The boat is scheduled to leave this evening, just after dark. My instructions were specific for the amount paid, with an evening departure at slow speed until at least 15 miles off the coast."

"Okay I got the plan and it sounds good to me," I said with some reservation. Can I pull this off?

An hour later...

Walking towards the dock, there wasn't much exchanged between the two of us. Helen did reach out and hold my hand, which was somewhat comforting. I was nervous as crud considering this wasn't the norm for a philosophy professor. I needed to keep cool and not allow this situation to get under my skin.

Approaching the boat dock, the familiar smell of diesel mixed with fish permeated the air. The tourist crowd also thinned, except the sparse fishing expeditions and scuba divers. I could detect a much rougher crowd of people than found in the city. Helen let go of my hand with these words: "Liam, the boat captain is going to perceive me as your traveling friend and nothing more. In his eyes, I'm just trash and of no value. You are the high value passenger," said Helen.

"Got it."

Helen presented me with a little drawstring bag and said, "The transaction is to occur in the galley of the boat. Don't pull out this bag until then. I see the boat right over there, the "Maria Cielo.""

Approaching the boat, it appeared to be at least thirty years old, with wear and tear from the ocean, including barnacles. Not sure what $200K would buy us for accommodations, but my expectations needed to be kept to myself. Helen spotted a few men on deck and provided a wave to get their attention. They pointed to the stairs aft of the boat to gain access to the deck. Well, this was it, and I was shaking inside but needed to have enough self-control somewhere between a coward and hero to get past this.

I took the lead up the stairs with the role of important passenger with Helen as my hired hand. She abided, understanding that posturing is needed in front of these drug runners. As we got to the deck, the men immediately said something in Spanish, and Helen answered back. They directed us to a door that I could assume was the location to meet the captain. Inside the boat, the dank smell and oily air were stifling. Considering this boat was exposed inside and outside to the elements, it was not a five-star ocean liner.

Helen and the crew exchanged a few words, and I expected she mentioned to them that she was my interpreter because their attention shifted. They led us down a poorly lit corridor and motioned us into a small room, which appeared to be the galley. We both were instructed to sit down, and one of the crew remained by the door, which I assumed was to guard us. No indication from the crew that this VIP person—me—was going to pay $200K for passage but more like expressions of a foreign dog condemnation.

"Liam, you okay?" whispered Helen.

"Yes, I'm fine. Anything I need to know?"

"No, we are doing fine and tracking. One of the crew is off to fetch the captain.

"Okay, got it," I said, keeping in mind her warning to minimize any talking.

"Hola," said a burly man as he entered the galley. I did not expect a warm welcome from the captain, but he appeared quite friendly and immediately put out his hand for me to shake. He completely ignored Helen, but she iterated something in Spanish that he acknowledged. I would expect she told him this gringo had no Spanish skills and that she was my translator.

Helen, being very tactful while speaking with the captain, appeared to have everything under control.

Helen reached over, nudged me, and at the same time said to me, "We are ready for the exchange."

I pulled out the bag of diamonds and handed it to the captain as he iterated, "Gracias," and smiled. He did not open the bag, and I assumed with the crew around, he would keep his jewels to himself. He did shake the bag a bit and would probably head back to his cabin and marvel at his take. Shortly, the captain spoke to the men standing guard and conveyed instructions to Helen.

"Liam, we are done here, and they will take us to our cabin below deck."

I think Helen was telling me to keep it tight and don't say anything to close the deal. We moved along the corridor with the two men, who looked like they had both lived hard lives. Each wore long sleeves, oily and dirty shirts along with jeans. Life on a boat running drugs I could imagine wasn't an admirable life in comparison to their fate of living in poverty in some forsaken place in South America. The users of drugs feed an endless cycle of crime, killings, and people churning through the cartels to maintain the flow to Western countries. No matter what intervention was taken by governments or the military, the western demand kept the flow of drugs moving. Just another demise this planet has to deal with and the associated value people place on the use of drugs for pleasure.

The two convict-looking crew members dropped us off in a room that had two mattresses on the floor and what appeared to be a toilet in a box. I was not sure if this was the stateroom of the ship, but it would have to do for the diamonds we exchanged.

Immediately, when the door shut, Helen reached over with a big hug and said, "Great job, Liam!"

"Thanks," I said with contemplation. Thinking what the hell would be next on this journey?

CHAPTER 14 ⚡ MENTAL TRAINING

Helen and I settled into our cozy room on the drug-lord ship. In spite of the accommodations, it was nice being here with her. I couldn't view any concerns from her with the situation. That's one thing I admired in this girl: adaptive, not complaining, and steadfast moving forward. I didn't expect any woman I had prior in my life would give up her cozy world to commit to such a mission. Then again, neither would any of my male friends, including the rugged ones. Most people are wrapped up in comforts and deliberately remove themselves from any mental challenges. If Helen and I were going to change or save the world, then I needed to toughen up and deal with these hardships.

"Hey, Liam, which mattress would you like tonight—the green one with stripes or the blue one with oil spots?" laughed Helen.

"Ahhh…I guess, being a gentleman, I will go with the blue one with the random oil spots," I laughed in return.

"Good choice," said Helen.

As we settled down, Helen made sure our packs remained close by. Considering we never knew if we would need to make a quick exit. It was best not to let our guard down. We took out limited supplies and left the rest in place for a possible quick dash.

Helen moved over to the door and slowly turned the latch to look around. All I heard was a "Hola," which most likely meant someone was on the other side watching us. I would suspect the ship captain didn't want the two of us wandering around his ship. If I were in his shoes, I would do the same and provide a guard to keep an eye on us.

Helen put her finger to her lips and said, "Whatever you say, don't trust we won't be overheard or that they don't understand English."

"Will do," I said without hesitation, since Helen was the boss when it came to keeping us safe.

"It's best we just lay low for a bit until we get out to sea," said Helen.

As we settled down for our departure, it was nice that the interior of the ship was slightly cooler than outside. Considering the age of this ship, I was surprised it even had some level of air-cooling. The room was damp with moisture, but that was to be expected in this humid environment. Helen pulled out a few snacks from our backpacks, and we had what amounted to dinner. Not sure what this luxury drug ship would be serving for cocktails and hors d'oeuvres tonight.

"Liam, just for reference, I estimate it will take us nine to ten days to reach our destination off the coast of northern Colombia. We will need to conserve our supplies, and I will talk with the crew so we can get food and provisions at least twice a day," said Helen.

"Colombia!" I exclaimed with a surprise.

"Yes, Colombia is our next stop. But no further discussion on our next stop," Helen said.

Well, not sure if she let the Colombia slip, but best not to make a big deal of things. However, nine to ten days on this freighter was for sure not going to be a treat.

"Okay, sounds good. Now two meals a day will be a challenge for me," I said with some contemplation of hunger pains.

"The key is to drink plenty of water and reserve our energy from here out," instructed Helen.

"So are we expected to remain trapped in this room for the entire trip?"

"No, but let me do some relationship building with the crew. They don't trust us, and likewise, we shouldn't trust them, so we need to build a bridge of communication," Helen said.

That made sense—let Helen do the conversing with the crew in Spanish to gain some level of trust. I needed to remember the norm in most countries is slow relationship building, not the fast-paced, let's get to know each other and get down to business. What is referred to as a friend in some parts of this world is more than that virtual person one meets while having online conversations. As a kid, I had many playmates, overnight visits, and trips outdoors and to the movies. However, somewhere the equation changed, and less face time and more texting had replaced companionship. Being here with Helen was awesome, and the last several days had been an amazing adventure. I knew that I was with someone who had at least five lifetimes over me, but she didn't come off condescending. It was more like, here we are in the present, and we need to live for the moment and survive with the tools we have at our disposal.

"Liam, are you good with coming over to the green mattress for some cuddling?" asked Helen.

"Yeah, for sure, Helen," sliding myself over to be next to her.

I held Helen, and I could feel her relax, with tension rolling out of her mind. Whatever she was holding back was a burden that only she could bear. I just needed to give her some quiet time, and in turn, I needed the same. We slowly drifted off to sleep...

Several hours later....

We both awoke from a good rest, and after that long bus ride, including a hustle to get on the boat that was a nice relief. Helen woke with a smile on her face.

"Helen, may I say something?" I asked.

"Sure."

"You look great, and I'm sure glad to be here with you."

"Liam, somehow we were brought together, and I'm feeling the same way," Helen said as she gave me a hug. "I'm going to check with our guard, but considering what time it is, we should be far out to sea," Helen said.

"Yes, it's great to finally be on the way," I said, considering we were making forward progress.

I would expect by looking at my watch that it was probably dark outside, even though our room had no windows and was located in the bowels of the ship.

"Helen, it would sure be nice if we could get some fresh air," I said.

"Agreed. Let me see what I can do for us."

Helen made her way to the door and knocked first to give the guard a heads up in case he was sleeping. I wouldn't have thought of this, but then again, most professors don't spend their time on drug boats out in the middle of nowhere. I could hear her conversing with the guard in Spanish and caught a laugh, so that was a good sign. The door opened wider, and Helen motioned to me to let go.

"Liam, I got us some topside but we need to hustle just in case he changes his mind," said Helen.

We followed the guard through the corridor and up several landing steps to reach the deck. I could see that it was dark outside, and just a few dim lights lit the ship. I would guess that a drug boat needed to be somewhat stealthy cruising the shipping lanes. The night air was quite refreshing after being confined in the damp interior of the ship.

The guard parked us on the aft of the boat on some wooden crates, and then he moved off to a single lifeboat hanging by ropes from the frame of the ship. This must be the smoking area since he immediately lit up with another individual sitting on a battered folding chair.

"Liam, we need to discuss our next move," said Helen.

Helen's tone of voice told me it was time to be serious. "Okay, I'm all ears."

"First, we have at least nine days at the anticipated speed before we near the Colombian coast. At that time, we will make our move to divert any attention from where we are heading."

"What do you mean?" I asked.

"In due time, Liam. There is something we both have to do. Remember, we discussed that at some point in time there may be a need for drastic measures to ensure we get to our destination undetected."

"Yes, but what do you have in mind?" I asked again.

"Hold that thought. I need a little more time to work out the details in my head."

"Okay," I said with a mental smirk. When she was ready, like usual, she would lay out the plan.

"Liam, remember we talked about the Planters, Producers, and Evolvers?" said Helen.

"Yes, I sort of remember."

"Let me add more connectivity for you."

"Okay."

"First, many millennia ago, the Planters provided enhancements of DNA to your species. At that point in time, the dominant species of humankind was ready to spread its wings. Our Planters spread new DNA seeds across the continents as part of the growth plan."

"So should humankind consider we're not unique?" I asked.

"Not at all, the DNA was to provide a basis for survival and growing your species. The galaxy collective is built on the value of life and the growth of immature species."

"All right, sort of makes sense carry on," I said with my normal trepidation while listening to Helen.

"The DNA mix provided several enhancements, including brain growth, human physique, and creativity to start the process of development. Our next effort was with the Producers, who again spread themselves out to provide growth across the continents. Remember, we are only a few individuals who focus on small tweaks over many years to ensure an outcome."

"Not to be asking too many questions, but why only a few people of your kind?" I asked.

"Good question, Liam, and I'm okay with you asking. The effort of our kind is based on providing slow and systematic change in species. It only takes a few people with a steady push to compound the effects over time. So our kind designates a contingency of replication that a few of us may fail to accomplish our mission," Helen said with a level of concern on her face.

"Helen, you are an Evolver, and from what you told me, the rest of you may have been lost."

"Yes, that is true, Liam, and I hope you understand how critical our mission is and how you play into the outcome."

"Yes, it's starting to make a lot of sense, please continue."

"The Producers' position and mission is to move the species out of the hunter-gatherer environments into farming, townships, governments, and cultures. A species left in the mode of hunter-gatherer can't, over the long term, survive the elements of the planet and grow in sophistication."

"Okay, I can buy that, but wouldn't that just happen spontaneously for a civilization by the process of creating a community culture?" I asked.

"To some degree yes, but civilization is based on probability of an outcome and sustained growth without self-destruction. Having a basis to grow and develop is time dependent on getting over the hump to ensure survivability against conflicts, weather, natural disasters, diseases, and other plights. Think of the odds of life and evolution when there are so many factors against it."

"I guess we take all of our past for granted when we turn on our television and have a refrigerator full of food," I said with contemplation.

"Exactly. You forget what it took to get to this point in human civilization. The Producers' role was to provide the humans the push in culture, organization, spiritual faith, government, and other aspects most people today just forget were years in the making," said Helen.

"Okay, that sounds all great, but what about the DNA from the Planters?"

"Well, that is where the story gets interesting. Consider when humans were tribal on the savannah in small groups fending for themselves. Their DNA mix was quite limited, constrained by distance and the inability to intermingle. The Producers' position is creating more human infrastructure. The probability of DNA mix and mutations would increase with people engaging across nations and continents. This was key in the start of a chain of events that would increase populations, genetic diversity, and linking of humans across regional environments."

"Wow, I never thought of that. So essentially, having a larger DNA mix would create mutations and strengthen the human populations," I said with amazement.

"Exactly. Our purpose on this planet has been to create steady change in the species and grow civilization's odds over failure or collapse. All very positive to some degree," said Helen with a look of concern as she considered the consequences.

"Helen, all true, but look at where we are at today with wars, crime, dysfunctional leadership, egomaniacs, and other chaotic situations. Where does that all fit in?" I asked.

"In due time, I will explain the next phase in humankind, which lies with the Evolvers. You are correct that the world populations started by the producers have increased exponentially, and along with that comes proximity of human contact, frustrations, wars, conflicts, and other dark elements of the human expansion process," said Helen.

"Not a pretty picture for sure, and what can we do?" I asked.

"Truthfully, nothing—the pendulum was anticipated to swing in the negative direction. This is the predictable outcome of most civilizations as they expand, consume more, desire more, and collectively come to this point."

"Again back to the question, what is the end game if left to its own accord?"

"Liam, the outcome is the de-evolution of your civilization," Helen said with the utmost seriousness.

"But Helen, humans have survived countless wars, pestilence, and global calamities, and you're telling me we are at the edge of our own survivability?"

"Liam, you are correct, but those events were only a few cards on the table. Now the world's connected resources are overstretched; the rise of malcontent is prevalent in people, governments, and growing consumption. Think of a future when the electricity goes off and grocery stores no longer have food stocked. What do you think will happen?"

"Humans would most likely implode in just a few weeks," I said.

"Would humans ever recover and start the cycle again to build a new civilization? Possibly, but think if we could provide those left behind with a better chance by stacking the deck."

"Like what I asked?"

"I'm going to give you something to think about. Is it intelligence, physique, technology development, or something else that you would consider the next step in human evolution?" Helen asked.

"Good question. I would say all of the above," I said.

"Liam, hold my hand for a moment." As I reached out to hold Helen's hand, I could feel the warmth of her inside me, and it felt wonderful.

"Liam, what do you feel?"

"Your heart inside me is the best way to describe it," I said.

"You have touched evolution. We call it empathy," Helen said. I let go of Helen's hand and was taken by surprise by the words she provided.

"Empathy...what are you talking about?" I said, deeply confused.

"Yes, empathy is what evolution is all about. Think of a society that didn't live on greed, bigotry, hate, abuse, and envy but instead has empathy towards others. Paint a picture in your mind of a civilization that didn't need to draw imaginary borders and had mindfulness to live together rather than behind fences," said Helen.

"Hard to imagine considering how screwed up the world is today and heading," I said.

"Exactly. Ask yourself how you would fix today's divisions of religion, ideals, governments, and on and on. Then consider the chaos and entropy that is growing as populations expand and resources are consumed at a faster rate, and I think you get the picture," said Helen.

"Es hora de ir debajo de la cubierta," said the boat guard.

"Sí, estamos listos," said Helen in response. "Liam, we need to head back. Looks like our guard has finished with his smoking buddies."

"Okay," I said to Helen. "Just one more question. You're getting me ready for something, aren't you?"

"Yes, that's the idea," said Helen as we walked quietly in front of the guard back to our room.

Preparing for something and building my thoughts towards that event was what Helen was providing. I think if she fed me all the information at one time, I wouldn't be able to fully absorb it. Something was changing in the world with the two nuclear explosions. These events triggered riots, financial instability, and global suspicion. In my mind, things went from okay to downtrodden. Whoever was pulling the strings had an evil mission in mind and nothing good for the planet.

As we approached our holding room, I felt a cold chill come over me. I knew that in spite of what Helen had told me, there was darkness in this world that lurked in the background. I have read where one percent of the population controls thirty-nine percent of the wealth. Not that I hold anything against the wealthy, but the power that resides within those hands could have implications for the rest of us. If it comes down to survival, there is potential for decisions that contribute to dealing with the masses. I could paint a picture in my mind that the nukes were not a terrorist plot but instead were meant to turn the world upon itself. Something terrible was going on.

"You look ready for bed," said Helen.

"For sure. I'm just beat after a long day, and ships aren't my best friend."

"Well, how about a little cuddling to maybe help you forget?" asked Helen.

"Great idea," I said.

As I laid there holding Helen, I felt her warmth; evolutionary compassion of empathy was more than just words from her. I now knew she had empathy on her mind for humankind, but what aspects of change did she have in mind? I needed to give my mind a rest—we had several more days on this ship to get ourselves fully aligned.

"Good night, Helen."

"Buenas noches."

CHAPTER 15 ⚇ COLOMBIA

It had been several days, and we had to be closing in on the coast of Colombia. Helen had been very gracious on this trip, including social engagements with the crew. They had allowed her to roam freely around the ship, which I was sure had some purpose for her. For me, spending most of the time just hanging out in the room or short stints on the upper deck had been challenging. Stripped of my basic needs, including the Internet, a fridge full of food, and my widescreen television, had induced mental withdrawal symptoms. Nevertheless, in turn, I was thinking more clearly, not influenced by every marketing scheme or overload of information from the media. Hell, I didn't even know if the world still existed considering we had zero communication with the outside.

Weight-wise I must have lost at least five pounds with the lack of my normal fast food snacks. As for Helen, she had become even more beautiful on this trip. Spending more time on the upper deck, her skin had taken on a nice copper bronze of beauty. Her hair even lightened a bit with the exposure to the tropical sun. I cherished every moment with her, and she had, in turn, reciprocated with kindness. She put my needs in front of her own when it came to meals and quiet times. This could be just the calm before the storm, though, and maybe her message to me was 'Get some rest, my friend; you have no idea what is ahead of us.'

"So what's on the agenda for today, Helen?"

"Tonight we are going to sink this boat," Helen said with a blank expression.

"What?" I said with a less than mild surprise.

"Yes, we are going to sink this boat."

"Why—and what the flip for?" I asked.

"Liam, you probably noticed our old age look is wearing off. In several days, we will be back to normal, and the possibility of being detected increases."

"Well yeah, but what does that have to do with sinking the fricking boat?"

"A lot. Think of the sequence of events. The entire crew is becoming suspicious watching our outward appearance changing. In addition, they will remember us in every minute detail," said Helen.

"So what about us and the crew?"

"Liam, remember when I said at some point in time drastic actions would have to be taken on this mission?" said Helen.

"Yeah, sort of."

"Well, that time has come, and this is when we have to put right and wrong aside to ensure we complete the mission."

"All right, feed me some logic, Helen," I said with a tight upper lip. Helen could see I was already putting up a defense.

"Well, you probably noted there is only one life boat on this ship and that is where we will be when the ship sinks beneath the waves. I also found two inflatable rafts and have already damaged them beyond any possible repair," Helen expressed with a sigh of content.

"But what about the crew?"

"Liam, they won't be coming with us," said Helen in a solemn voice.

"Not coming with us! So like where will they be heading?" I asked.

Helen reached out to hold my hand and said, "Liam, they are going down with the ship."

"Wait! Where is the evolutionary empathy in killing all the crew?" I stammered, pulling my hands away.

"There is none—we have to cover our tracks, and the stakes at this time don't include saving the lives of the crew."

My mind was racing. This was the last thing I would have suspected coming out of Helen. It was always about growing and preserving life with her, and now she wanted the two of us to take out twenty people on a drug boat. I didn't sign up for this!

"I would like you to reflect for a moment on all our discussions, from the time we met at the café in Idaho to where we are today."

I hesitated to think back, but my training as a philosophy professor was replaced with my immediate thought of killing twenty innocent drug runners. Well, not so innocent when it came to what they were doing. Nerveless, this was something way beyond my normal ethical and moral obligations I had encountered while meandering through life.

"Okay, Helen carry on," I said with contemplation.

"The world is at a pivotal moment. Survival of the fittest won't necessarily guarantee evolutionary change. In addition, the question of de-evolution is a probability with the position of weapons, splintered countries, global pollution, resource depletion, and, of course, uncontrolled population growth. The reality is we have to finish the mission to allow evolution a chance for survival of your species."

I took a deep breath. Everything she had said was within the logic of what I should comprehend. Still, the question lingered on of wiping out twenty men for our own needs.

"I know you're struggling, but look at me, Liam. We have to do this. If we don't cover our tracks every step of the way, we are easy targets, which includes being killed ourselves," said

Helen with a look that conveyed the seriousness of the situation.

"Helen, I'm in a quandary, and I know you're telling me something that resides in reality, but my mind just doesn't want to accept it."

"Of course not, Liam, but consider my position as an Evolver—centuries of work to reach this point. I'm possibly the last of my kind to make the decisions, and I need you all the way with me."

"Helen, my time has come to step up to the plate, hasn't it?" I asked.

"Yes, it has Liam," said Helen as she looked deep into my eyes.

"What's the plan so we can get started?" I said, knowing I would have to hold the pain inside my mind forever. If the planet was at a pivot point, I think this was mine. Considering the short time I had spent with Helen and what we had talked about, the world currently in turmoil had to be a message. This was my time to grow some courage beyond the city boy that resided in my personality.

Looking back to Helen, she continued with "Well, first, tonight we should be within miles of the coast of Colombia. Where exactly I don't know, but close enough for us to reach shore. I will need you to get the lifeboat into the water, and I will take care of the rest."

"What is take care of the rest?"

"Over the last several days I have placed three explosive charges I have been carrying in my backpack I procured in Magdalena. I have placed all of them on bow and stern weak points that should create a quick flooding of the hull's compartments."

"Okay, but how can I get to the lifeboat without being spotted?" I said.

"Not to worry. I will take out the night watchmen for you," said Helen.

No need to enquire how Helen would take out the guards; she was capable enough. In the end, the entire crew was going to the bottom of the ocean.

"There won't be much time or many chances to get the lifeboat in the water. At most, you have five minutes when the charges explode and the crew figures out what is going on. The mechanism is simple—you just need to release the rope clamps on the bow and stern; then the single rope with a pulley will allow the boat to swing over the side into the ocean. The key is to not drop the boat too quickly or we will lose it," said Helen.

"Okay, I got the simple part. What's next?" I asked.

"Next, you jump over the side of the ship, swim to the lifeboat, and wait for me."

This was starting to sound like I had the least amount of effort to scuttle the boat, but as I once heard from someone, "All plans are great until you fire the first bullet." Gosh, sure hoped that I could pull off everything Helen was asking of me since it was either them or us at this time. If those charges went off and we weren't in a position to get away, they would surely kill us.

"I know you can do this, and I have confidence in you." Helen smiled.

"All I know, Helen, is that I'm not leaving without you!"

"Not to worry. We have a great chance of making it while most of the crew is sleeping. I only have to deal with a few men, and before they can react, the ship should be flooded."

I was considering asking where Helen got her hands on the explosives, but it was probably not worth my time. Considering she smuggled me across the border, explosives were most likely within her skill set.

"Helen, can I ask you a question?"

"Sure, go ahead."

"What would the nun Helen have to say about what we are doing?"

"She would say, The Meek Shall Inherit the Earth," Helen said with some hidden meaning covering her expression.

Hmmm…I could not quite agree with Helen on that point, but that had to mean something. I could only hope that down the road all this chaos would come to some meaningful point. I could reflect back on sitting at the Starbucks at the local grocery store grading papers and watching people wander through the infinite rows of food with their baskets filled with all the treats that make eating delightful. However, behind the scenes were the people, trucks, infrastructure, and all the other items that moved that food into the grocery store. What would we do if we woke up one day and all the items we take for granted were gone? Would we quickly degrade into a state of chaos and territorial barbaric behaviors and then finish each other off with sticks and stones? I would hope that somewhere in that equation the meek would have a chance to survive and rebuild a better world.

"Are you ready to roll?"

"Yeah, I have your back—let's do it," I said with probably the fullest commitment of conviction I have ever had in my life!

Helen opened the door carefully, smiled at the guy watching us, and then unleashed a kick to his face that brought him down. The kick was lighting fast, before he could react.

"Grab his legs, and we need to drag him inside and gag him," said Helen with her commanding voice.

I tied his hands and feet and stuffed his mouth with a rag and rope to ensure it wouldn't come out. I figured I might as well cover his head so if anyone took a quick peek he would be ignored.

"Liam, we have to move fast. Don't forget you will need to carry both our packs to the lifeboat!" Helen said as she turned, gave me a quick good luck kiss, and was off down the corridor.

I was now on my own for essentially the first time on this mission without Helen. I couldn't hesitate but needed to execute and stop thinking like my life still resided in Moscow, Idaho. Walking the corridors while everyone was sleeping had an uneasy peace since one slip-up and I would have a bunch of guys with knives and guns all over me in spite of the cash we had paid for passage to Colombia. I had to slowly get up the steps—damn, didn't remember this many squeaks while climbing them during the daytime.

Ahhh, finally, there's the exterior door. Okay, slowly turn the lever and look around as instructed by Helen. Frick—there is someone pacing the deck. There was no way I could take out this beefy guy; I would just need to huddle on the deck until he was on the other side and then slip over to the lifeboat. Whoa, my heart is racing, and I could feel my adrenaline churning inside me. I felt alive for the first time in my life, which in a strange way, was awesome.

Great he is moving along—now I could make my move over to the lifeboat. Watch check—crud, I only have five minutes and Helen is going to blow the charges. Scooting along low to the deck was probably best. Okay, flip open the lifeboat cover per the mental rehearsal with Helen and put backpacks in the bow of the boat safe so as not to lose them overboard. Wait, my task was to lower the boat into the water, but flip, the ship is moving. Hell, I had never done this, and once those charges went off, if Helen and I weren't on the lifeboat, we were dead. Okay, I would just skip the lifeboat down along the edge of the ship then make the drop when I see Helen. Crud, the deck guard is coming. Whoa, that was close, but the boat cover should shield me while he passes.

Two minutes to get this boat over the side. Peeking outside, all was clear, so it was time to release the boat over the side quickly. Since this was an old-school lifeboat, I needed to release the rope pulleys first then manhandle both ropes to get this girl moving. Ahhh…not that bad, moving fairly well, and there was the water. Frick, there were the charges, and wow, that is going to wake up the entire flipping ship.

"Oh mi dios nos estamos hundiendo!" Shouts could be heard.

"Bastardo qué demonios estás hacienda." The deck guard was glaring down at me with his rifle ready to fire!

Whoa where in the frick did he go? A major scuffle on the deck commenced, and a gun went flying over the side.

"Liam, I'm coming down. Get ready to release the boat fast," Helen said as I could hear bullets being fired.

With one swoop, Helen grabbed a deck rope and jumped down to me as I released the final pulley to let the boat hit the water. Both of us without hesitation jumped over the side of the ship and made no time boarding the lifeboat. Thank God we both made it okay!

The ship still had momentum as we started to fall behind the stern as bullets passed over our heads. Our timing was good, since there was not a full moon tonight and darkness covered our escape as the ship slipped farther away. Both Helen and I watched as the drug ship capsized, and hearing the screaming men wasn't pleasant knowing they didn't have the time to save themselves. Within seconds, all was quiet except the shallow sound of the waves against the sides of our lifeboat.

Helen reached over to me and said, "Liam, my heart is in the same place."

"Yeah, I'm not doing that well myself right now," I said with the deepest despair.

"How about we give them a moment of silence," said Helen as she sat next to me and reached down to hold my hands. I could feel her hands ripped open from the rope burns and I knew she was in pain, but she still reached out to hold me anyway. Sitting here in this lonely spot on the ocean, I felt empty right now despite having Helen next to me. I knew this girl had empathy for those men, but there had to be some higher order that had to be fulfilled for humankind and I hoped my strength held up to see it to the end.

CHAPTER 16 ♄ FLIGHT FOR SURVIVAL

In the far off distance, I could at least spot a few dim lights that I hoped was the coastline. The sun should be peaking on the horizon shortly so we could gauge our position off the coast. Helen was still sleeping after a long night and the sinking of the drug ship. The plan had no survivors, and considering how fast the boat sank, I would think all of them went down with the ship. Unsettled thoughts continued to run through my mind. I probably would have this horrible night in my thoughts for the rest of my life. In addition, the consideration of what had to be done was pure insanity more than reality. Nevertheless, Helen was in charge, and she had asked me if I was in our out, so that choice ultimately was mine.

The first glimmer of light was starting to crest on the horizon. It was probably best to wake up

Helen so we could work together to get this old and battered boat heading in the right direction. I hoped that her repertoire of skills included sea navigation.

"Helen, Helen...time to rise," I said with a slow jostle of her shoulder.

"Well, looks like we made it," Helen said as she sat up and scanned across the ocean before us.

"Yes, and off to the east I think is the coast," I said with some questions about my own observations. Helen brought her attention to our position and said, "Yes, Liam, it looks like we did well on timing with the location on where the ship went down."

"So what's next?" I asked.

"Breakfast...why don't we check the packs?"

Rummaging through the packs, food and water were well stocked from our preparations. The problem was knowing where the next convenience store was to replace whatever we consumed. I pulled out a loaf of bread and some granola bars that should work with a couple of juice boxes. Helen and I both ate in silence as we listened to the waves and spotted a few high-flying sea birds circling on an early morning fish hunt. From all indications, we were drifting closer to shore, which was good news while we finished off our breakfast.

"Helen, not to ask a stupid question, but how do we plan on getting to shore?"

"Liam, under the bow should be a couple of paddles, which should get us close enough."

"I'm not sure what you mean by close enough," I said.

"Well, we are going to scuttle this boat. There's no way we can leave any trace of where we land or association with the ship we sunk."

Great, another boat sinking to add to my international criminal record. It wasn't as if we would need any explosive to take this boat out like the last one. However, the question remained of how to sink this boat—or dispose of it.

Helen grabbed the two paddles out of the hold of the boat located at the bow. She appeared to know what she was doing as she maneuvered each into the side sockets of the boat. Looking at me, she asked, "Ready to row?"

"Yes, let's get moving," I said while stuffing the residual trash into the backpack. I positioned myself on the seat next to the handle and grabbed the paddles with both hands.

"We need to coordinate to get the boat heading in the right direction. When I say pull right, you need to dig deep so we turn in the correct direction. I'll take the left."

As we started to work together, the boat slowly aligned under our coordination, and slowly moved towards the shore. I could now make out rocks, palm trees, and a white, sandy beach. At this rate, it would take us at least another thirty minutes of hard paddling to make it closer to shore.

"Pull right!" commanded Helen, and I dug deep into the waves to improve our forward direction. It looked like we were drifting with an undercurrent as we approached the shore. Rowing was not a primary asset on my personal strength portfolio, so I was struggling while Helen appeared to be steady. The way she took out the crew, I could consider her extraordinary in the endurance category.

"Liam, pull right. We're drifting too fast and will miss the landing spot," shouted Helen.

"Yes, I'm on it," I said, knowing she was right as I considered the surf was picking up as we approached land, and I could now spot coral underneath the boat.

"See that small patch of sand? That is our target and in about two minutes, we are going to scuttle the boat," said Helen in a state of urgency.

"How exactly are we going to do that?" I asked.

"First we will remove the bilge plug, and then when the boat is lower in the water, we'll rock it to ensure it fills with water and sinks."

"What do we do with the packs?" I asked again, ensuring we had all the bases covered with this plan.

"Liam, are you a strong swimmer?"

"I would call myself below average," I said, considering the last thing on my mind in Idaho was an Olympic swim to reach a beach.

"That's all right. If you can grab us two life vests under the bow, we can put those on. Then each of us can grab a pack and swim to the shore. How does that sound?" Helen asked.

"I'm good. Let's pull the plug," I said.

After putting on the life vest, I felt a lot more comfortable bailing out of the boat. We must have been at least 150 yards offshore, and truthfully, I was questioning my ability to make it. Swimming in the ocean, from my experiences, drained me quickly, and no way did I want to end up dead off the coast of Colombia. Helen pulled the plug, and water started entering the bottom much quicker than I expected.

"Liam, grab your pack. We're going over."

Grabbing my pack and jumping overboard was a bit of a chill but not that bad considering our location to the tropics. The pack wasn't easy to handle, but the life vest was doing a great job of keeping me afloat.

"Liam, grab the other side of the boat, and let's start rocking to get the boat filled and sunk before anyone catches a glimpse of us," said Helen.

As we started to rock the boat, it wasn't more than a few minutes and the end had come for our escape from the drug boat. It was somewhat melodramatic watching the boat slip under the waves, and a few items floated out, but nothing critical as it made its way to the bottom. Helen had taken every precaution possible to disconnect us from our transit to Colombia. Our facial features had transformed back from the old-age look, so that should help for a short period of time, but then again, who would pick up on our trail was a lingering question.

"Liam, kick with your feet, and hold onto the pack," Helen instructed, recognizing I was struggling with swimming.

"Yeah, got it," I stammered, working my way through the surf. It wasn't much farther, which was great since my legs were about to give up. Helen, in turn, was clipping along at a great pace like a veteran swimmer, which was a bit intimidating for me. This girl excelled in just about everything.

"We're near coral, and you could get cut up pretty bad, so watch out!" exclaimed Helen.

"Yes, got it," I said between my puffs of air as I struggled between the ocean lapping at my face and my weary legs keeping me moving forward. Finally reaching the bottom with my feet, I started pushing towards shore, following Helen. "Whew, that was just enough to freak me out," I said.

"Yes, that was sort of tricky, but it looks like we sunk the boat far enough out to keep it from moving," said Helen as she started her scan of our location.

"Can we just rest a bit?" I asked.

"Yes, let's move to the edge of the trees and dry off," said Helen.

Moving to the edge of the tree line, this place was beautiful, with large, weathered rocks, palm trees, and green everywhere. I had never been to this region of the world, but what a place. The weather was not too bad with a little overcast to provide some relief from the sun overhead. Yes, it would be nice to just settle down with a cool drink, sit back in a bungalow, and enjoy this beach with Helen. However, I knew this image would never be a long-term reality.

Helen undressed in front of me down to her underwear with no thought of me and hung her clothes on the low-hanging branches to dry out. She was all business since there was no time for much of anything else on this mission. In turn, I did the same with my clothes, although with a bit more modesty while looking at the beauty of Helen before me. I really liked her, no matter if my mind was saying no don't go down that path. She had brought me a spirit of being alive and not my former life attached to my remote and high-definition television.

"Liam, it's time we sit for a download," said Helen.

"Okay, what's up?" I asked.

"There is a good chance we have a slight lead on whoever is ever after us. Most likely they don't want us dead immediately. Since my four other members have possibly been terminated, I'm considering I'm the last one with the knowledge to reach the end of the mission."

"Okay, so what does that mean?" I asked with my normal state of confusion of what exactly was going on.

"Liam, I may be the only one on the planet who understands the end goal. Those others of my kind would have given up their lives to uphold the knowledge. My logic tells me they want what I know as the end goal," said Helen.

"So what exactly is that?"

"In due time, Liam. For now, let's keep that part in my head."

I knew compartmentalization was the norm for Helen, but unfortunately, it remained under her guard. Breathing deeply, I knew there was no way I could push her for more. Helen's verbal history was keeping it tight and providing me crumbs to keep things moving forward.

"In this technological world, no one can keep many things confidential for an extended period of time. Right now, there may be satellites looking for us, supercomputers, and artificial intelligence databases sifting through information to figure out where we are on this planet. Most likely multiple groups are working together to track us down."

"Yeah, I get all that, but what happens to us?" I asked.

"We delay them as much as possible, watch our tail, create distractions—whatever it takes to stay alive," said Helen as she gazed past me into the jungle.

An entire planet looking for two people didn't stack the odds well for us. Whatever our end goal was must have some impact on the planet; otherwise Helen wouldn't be giving me the lowdown on the consequences if we screwed up.

"So, Helen, do you have any idea where we are?" I said, hoping we weren't on another planet.

"Yes, we are in the Golfo Torgus of Colombia, from my last bearing at sea. Our crew was heading to a location near the city of Tumaco down the coast," said Helen.

"So I can assume we aren't near that spot on the coast?"

"Correct. We left the boat miles north of Tumaco."

"Probably not a bad idea and what is our next target?" I asked, hoping for an answer.

"Our target city is Buenaventura, Colombia, where we should be able to pick up some transportation. But prior to that, we have, from my estimate, around a ten to twelve mile hike along the coast."

Well, it could be worse. This place was beautiful, and some walking time with Helen probably wouldn't be a bad thing. The beach looked tranquil which was good for at least the time being.

"There are many local fishing villages scattered along the coast, and I expect someone will go for a few of the diamonds for a boat trip to Buenaventura," said Helen.

"That sounds great, and hopefully we can get some fresh supplies at this town we are heading to," I said, considering who knows what was in store for us.

"Yes, we should be able to get something, but don't plan on staying too long. Our only hope is to stay on the move and not be idle," Helen said, again scanning the horizon. "One more thing—the city of Buenaventura has a reputation for being one of the Colombia's highest crime cities, so we have to be vigilant," stated Helen.

Vigilant…if it wasn't for Helen, I don't think there is any way I would have made it this far. Caring for me along the way may be a burden for her, but I doubt she could have pulled off the boat caper by herself. I think that no matter what, she was at least respectful of my companionship.

"Helen, do you like me?" I blurted out.

"Liam that comes as a surprise question!"

Gosh, hope that wasn't out of place; it's not my normal opening conversation to get attention.

"Sorry just thinking about it."

"No reason to apologize. I'm going to tell you something from my heart. I'm mortally scared and wounded emotionally with the possible loss of my kind. I didn't just find you, but was guided to you."

"What do you mean?"

"In this infinite world of possibilities, some of us don't meet by chance but are guided like magnets. How I ended up in Idaho in that ragged home was my destiny, and you were also." Helen reached out to hold my hand, as she looked deep into my eyes.

There was no more that needed to be said between us. In her own way, Helen had told me how she felt about me. Like two kindred spirits, there was a reason for all of this, and the two of us being together was more than a coincidence. I needed to put aside my insecurities and do whatever it takes to protect and be a part of the mission to the end.

"Thanks, Helen. That is exactly how I feel. Is there anywhere in the world I would like to be today or with someone else…no. You are it," I said with an appreciative smile.

Helen smiled at me, and we connected closer, mind to mind and spirit like no one I had ever been with on this planet. Crud, I was starting to think like an off planet citizen sitting here with Helen. World, please keep spinning; I wanted this never to end with Helen.

"Liam, I think it's time we get dressed and head out before the day gets away from us."

"I agree. Let me grab our packs and sweep the sand with some palm branches to reduce our presence signature," I said.

"Good idea, and let's not wave at any of the overhead satellites that are probably on the prowl for the two of us," Helen laughed.

Grabbing our stuff and getting on with the walk along the beach was a good idea. Staying put too long only created more opportunity for detection. The sun was getting high in the sky and beating down on my head. My sneakers were quickly getting sand inside, but it was better than walking barefoot and making less progress with each step. I let Helen take point since she appeared to want it between the two of us. Probably not a bad idea, since her level of cognizance was much higher than mine was.

"Are you doing okay back there?"

"Yes, hanging in there," I said, well knowing my energy level was waning with every step. In the past, I enjoyed jogging, but lately I had been spending too much time idle on the couch, and it had its consequences. I probably should have considered having a regular workout schedule and eating better than the quick stops at the local drive-thru. It was just easier to just sit back in life and be sucked into the idle nature of mental input from the mass media. The world may be falling apart, but people are focused on what's the latest electronic gadget to fulfill their well-being. I remember reading the article that stated something like the world is nine meals away from anarchy—I needed to add that to Helen's equation for completing the mission.

"Helen, can I ask you a question?" I said, picking up the pace to catch up with her.

"Sure."

"How delicate are we living day to day?" I asked.

"Sorry, I don't understand your question."

"Well, I mean if there were just one blip in electricity or food supply, what do you think would happen?"

"Chaos would ensue with no recourse to recover. Governments and order would topple overnight, and the fierce would destroy the weak," said Helen.

"But how can you be so sure?"

"Liam, you live a very comfortable life in Idaho—you have your job, home, food, friends—but you know what? The rest of the world is struggling, shooting bullets at each other, and growing more restless," said Helen with a level of contemplation.

"Well yeah, but I have hope for humankind."

"I do also, but be realistic, how would you fix a technology downfall, catastrophic disaster, or world upheaval? You would resort to your natural instinct for survival. You would be up against people wanting to kill you for a few breadcrumbs, a gallon of gasoline—there is no option for them. A spontaneous community of well-being individuals isn't going to spring up with the current population's mindset," Helen said with a stern and commanding voice.

"Okay, then how is the mission going to play into the equation?" I asked as a counterargument.

"It's going to change the playing field for survival that humans don't have today! That's all I have to say on this topic. Now let's pick up the pace."

I think Helen slightly bit my head off for that conversational discourse. I had to agree with her on many points, but I wasn't confident I could create any change under the auspices of anarchy. Heck, just getting the trashcan out every Thursday was challenging. My reality was a dream among the seven billion people scraping out a life on this planet. Something has to shift, but what did Helen have in mind that was concluding soon? In my field, I like to consider options, but from what Helen was telling me, humans have run out of options, and we have to pay for our sins.

"Sorry, Helen, I didn't mean to touch a sore spot," I said.

"Liam, the clock is ticking, and there is a small window to finish the mission."

"Yeah, I fully understand," I said, knowing that paradise was an illusion here with Helen. Gosh, this place was beautiful and almost primordial with so much green. However, along the beach, the traces of humankind included the proverbial plastic water bottle and debris washed in from the sea. Every bit of trash has a start in the hands of some human, and this disgusting stuff eventually ends up on some pristine beautiful beach.

Several hours later…

"Liam, up ahead, looks like a spot of village life. Let's stop here for a moment and think this through. A couple of strangers walking along the beach will bring suspicion."

"Agreed, what do you have in mind?" I asked.

"It's time for you to lead. How does that sound?"

Whoa, leadership handing me the reins, now that was a surprise. Helen was asking me for my opinion, and that was somewhat weird.

"What, you want me to come up with a plan?"

"Yes, that's correct," said Helen with a serious tone.

"Well, first we have to be adamant we're not lost and that we need a boat to take us to Buenaventura. We will tell them we are hiking the coast of Colombia, and that's it."

"Okay, now look around 360 and observe the details for a few minutes," said Helen.

I slowly started the 360 scan of the area and noted the boats on the coast all appeared in better shape than I expected and not a lot of people were congregating outside the local huts. A few dogs were chained, while others appeared to be watching us. No kids were to be seen, which was somewhat weird.

"Well, Helen, several things are odd, like most the boats are new, no kids playing, and dogs chained and some running free," I said.

"Okay, not bad. So what does that tell you?" asked Helen.

"Truthfully, I can project several guesses but haven't a clue what is uncorked about this place," I said, feeling a little stupid.

"Well, you hit the right buttons, and most likely this is a coastal drug village and a staging area for someone," said Helen.

"Okay," I added, considering I had missed the obvious.

"We walk into that village as strangers, and it would be easier just to kill us rather than provide us a boat ride to Buenaventura," said Helen.

Whoa, that was thinking that would never have come out of my head. This was a landmine of a place in disguise that would have got both of us killed.

"Wow, Helen, the naive professor in me missed the connection," I said.

"Liam, centuries of living on this planet has taught me a few things. We are going to have to give this place a wide berth and be vigilant to not attract any attention."

"Agreed, and can I pass the torch to you on that decision?"

Helen smiled at me and said, "Yes, we need to head in the jungle at least a quarter of a mile then move parallel to the beach and around these guys. Just be aware, in the jungle are a few deadly elements. Watch where you step, listen, and don't touch anything before you look," Helen instructed.

Helen, the endless guide and protector, with a statement to cover every situation one could think of. As I looked into the dark jungle, my mind shifted to getting out alive. Being an amateur on the outdoors wasn't good for this trek into an unknown element of danger. I would allow Helen to lead since there was no way I would be able to gauge our direction or distance. I could imagine when the Europeans approached South America they had no idea of the challenges they would face trekking across the jungles. In turn, they brought total destruction to multiple cultures in spite of being held back many times by the chaos of the same place we were entering. I needed to keep pace with Helen and try not to get myself killed in this hostile environment.

Helen turned around and whispered, "Ahhh… Liam I can hear every twig you step on—walk soft and scoot as needed so we can be stealthy."

"Okay," I said quietly. I didn't think I was making that much noise, but if Helen said I was, then best to follow orders. Gosh, it was difficult enough walking down a dirt path, but here there was nothing but tropical plants, trees, ground debris, and centipedes to deal with. How people could scratch out a life in the jungle is way beyond me. It would take generations of trial and error along with death to create an existence in this place. Civilization sort of reached a peak in the jungle then went into stasis as a survival of the fittest lived and died in endless repetitive cycles. I guess in some ways, some could call this paradise, but after being a recipient of technology and civilization, I'm not sure if I could regress back to this lifestyle of existence.

Looking forward, Helen took a knee and motioned me to stop and do the same. I couldn't spot any danger, but Helen was much more alert. She motioned me with her finger not to say a word to her and to be quiet. Helen carefully rolled around, coming to me, and then stood up just for a second before the crack of a gunshot sliced through the air, and Helen was down. A bullet had found its mark…

CHAPTER 17 ⴲ PASSING

My mind shifted as the jungle engulfed my thoughts—the chaos, the shuffle, and Helen going down with a gunshot struck my reality as I clawed my way back from the shadows of confusion.

I dropped to my knees immediately and crawled to Helen's side. I could clearly see blood on her torso, as she lay there motionless. What should I do? Think, Liam, think. Looking over the jungle surroundings, I could not view anyone in our immediate vicinity—which didn't make much sense. I had clearly heard the shot, but it was as if the jungle had swallowed up whoever pulled the trigger.

Best to just keep quiet. Maybe they lost our trail or expected us to make the next move—which didn't include many options at this time. As I held Helen, she began to stir. "Liam, are you all right?"

"Yes, Helen, I'm fine," I said, thinking it was just like Helen to be thinking of me.

"Good, I've been hit, and we need to try to stop the bleeding."

My only first aid in my life was an occasional bandage with anti-bacterial ointment, yet here I was facing a gunshot wound. I carefully pulled Helen's shirt up over her side to witness a ghastly hole in her side and blood gushing out of it.

"Put pressure on it, and then I need you to make me a temporary compression bandage."

"We need to get you to a hospital," I said, shaking and falling apart emotionally.

"No, this is it for me, Liam. I have come as far as this trip had planned for me," said Helen in a weak voice.

I quickly pulled a sock out of my backpack and applied it to Helen's wound as she winced in deep pain. Luckily, I had an old towel, which, when ripped up, made a good wrap around Helen's slim waist. I could feel her continue to weaken as I applied what little comfort I could provide.

Helen slowly pushed herself up against a tree mound with my help to a sitting position. The blood continued to expand in spite of my meager first aid, which concerned me—how would I ever get her out of the jungle?

"Liam, it's time."

"Time for what?"

"Time for the final story I need to convey to you," said Helen.

No way. This couldn't be the end. I didn't want the final story no matter what it was. I wanted Helen with me and not to be alone here in the Colombian jungle without her.

"Liam, I want you to remove your mind from me. What I'm going to convey is more important than my bleeding. So be quiet and clear your head."

Helen placed her hand by a spot next to her for me to sit down and held my hand as she began to tell me what I knew would be the truth behind the mission.

"I will try to keep this short, but every element is important. There are three waves of my kind: the Seeders, Producers, and Evolvers. I'm an Evolver and the last of my kind with the potential loss of my other associates. The Seeders came to the planet to alter the DNA to start the human race down a path of growth; the Producers brought the collective of what you today call civilization."

"Okay, but…" I said, thinking she had iterated this to me prior. Helen's weakened state and fear of dying was obvious as she spoke in pain.

"Liam, listen, no more interruptions. I don't have much time left. I'm an Evolver, which is the final part of our mission. The Producers increased the opportunity for the human population to expand, brought new life to the planet, and increased in collective well-being. The Evolvers of my kind were to ensure the populations increased exponentially for one element—evolution of the kind you wouldn't consider. Your evolution is what only a small portion of the population will experience, and it's not about intelligence, science, or technology. It's about empathy."

I looked deeply into Helen's eyes, knowing what she would be telling me next would change my world. She held my hand tighter, and her face continued to show signs of fading.

"Most likely I was shot and wounded so that what you hear next will be inside your head. They will continue to pursue you, and it's your choice to continue the mission, provide them the information I tell you, or whatever, since I won't be here to guide you. It's estimated that only less than 10% of the human population possesses true empathy. The rest have limited and mixed commitment to this deep element that is part of the human evolutionary path," said Helen.

My mind was racing and detached from Helen's thoughts. In all my academic training, evolution was considered the development of intelligence.

"The first path for humans was to attain intelligence to grow into the civilization you have today, but in order to avoid self-destruction and de-evolution, the aspect of empathy must be paramount for your survival. It's sort of like 'The Meek Shall Inherit the Earth.' The fact is, those meek are the population with empathy," said Helen, wiping her brow of the sweat trickling down.

"Helen, let me get you a bottle of water."

"No, Liam, just listen, and no more interruptions please," Helen stammered as she fought with her last efforts of energy. "We needed to exponentially increase the human population of the earth, in order for the random DNA mix to grow the population of Earth with empathy. Your kind has spread across this planet, in chaos mode to bring the next phase in your evolution. But the consequences of this growth included wars, discriminations, tribal fiefdoms, and, of course, the latest wave of nuclear explosions intended to bring about an economic collapse and global destruction never seen by this planet."

I wiped my hand across Helen's brow and continued to listen.

"You remember my paper on forest burning? Well, it's time for the earth's controlled burn, or the meek shall perish and the future of Earth will never flourish to join the galactic civilizations. I know this sounds incredulous, but that is the bottom line of what brings us to this point."

Helen coughed up blood, which wasn't a good sign, and she was extremely pale as I wiped her mouth clean. There was no way I could move her.

"In Machu Picchu, you will find a rock face with five bumps that look completely out of place. No one has ever figured out why the bumps are there. We figured the humans would just find them amusing. They are actually the code key that ends this mission. The activation sequence is from right to left; touch each one individually for one to two seconds. Once that is done, push the center three bumps from left to right just once, step back, and the mission is done," said Helen.

"Helen, what the hell will this do?" I said with a feeling of panic setting in.

"Liam, this sequence will release an invisible cloud of a DNA-encoded virus that will allow the meek to inherit the earth," said Helen.

"Wait. What are you talking about?" I said.

"Liam, the virus will spread from the people visiting Machu Picchu across the planet with an incubation period of two weeks and impact those that would otherwise end the future of this planet."

"That is genocide!" I said as Helen interrupted me.

"Liam, you are here for a reason. Now calm down, and listen to me," stammered Helen.

My composure was waning as I watched Helen's life slip away as I was asked to purge the population of Earth. This reality was way outside of my moral compass to carry out.

"The choice lies on your shoulders. I can't tell you or promise that the virus won't kill you once it's released. You will be a carrier just like everyone else at Machu Picchu when the event transpires, but let me paint a picture of how the world can flourish. When the two weeks pass, there will be a loss of the population and grief among the survivors but not turmoil, chaos, or fear among those left behind. Those left behind will have the gift of evolution we call empathy and will start to band together, pull their resources together, and start down a path of carrying and loving each other. The element of the population that would carry greed, self-centeredness, hate, and demise won't be around to hold back the meek as they inherit the earth," gasped Helen as more blood and coughing continued between her words.

I reached over to Helen and said, "Helen, I love you," holding her tightly, knowing she couldn't do the same.

"The time has come to tell you goodbye, Liam. I love you more than you realize," Helen said with her last breath as her body fell limp in my arms.

I lay Helen down on the ground, shaking emotionally and physically. My mind couldn't fully bear the pain I felt inside as I knelt down and tears poured from my face for the woman who was the most amazing, wonderful person I had ever met. The perspective of my life was meaningless as I held back more tears, considering someone could have a bullet sight on me as the next victim. Nevertheless, if Helen's logic were correct, they would let go as a pawn in the equation of the hunted. What I held inside my head right now was the most dangerous thinking that the world could bear.

I needed to pull myself together and consider Helen's passing and my survival. Helen gave her life for humankind and me. No matter what happened now, I was essentially a dead man either way. If I finished the mission, I could die; if I gave myself up, the truth would be tortured out of me, and then I would probably be shot. I would think Helen realized this as I closed both of her eyes and she viewed mine for the last time.

My best option was to stay quiet and hope whoever was out there would give me a pause to collect my wits. It was probably best to place jungle branches on Helen and move towards the city of Buenaventura. I had to remember and retain everything Helen told me down to the details of moving forward. As I placed branches and leaves on Helen, I could feel emotional remorse tearing my heart apart.

Finishing up, I had to consider I would never return to this place. Helen would never see a proper burial, and maybe it was best to silently provide the words that I knew she would hear as she watched over me.

Okay…where to start? I whispered silently,

"Helen, I lay you down to rest in this far off land.

Please forgive me for any burdens I set forth.

My heart and love will always be with you.

You are the spirit that will carry me forward.

If not for you, my life would be a worthless waste.

You gave me a new heart, courage, and determination.

At this moment, I know you're still with me…somewhere.

I love you, my best friend, companion, and giver of your soul.

Empathy is now my mission I will carry out to the end…

Placing the last set of branches and giving Helen a kiss on her forehead was my last goodbye. Looking around, I couldn't view nor detect any movement out in the jungle. If someone was watching me, I was just too stupid and emotionally wrecked to be cognizant of anyone out there. I just hope I didn't screw up my last bearing on direction since going deeper into the jungle would be deadly for me. I needed to get back to the coast as my best chance of making it to the city.

Bugs, flies, and mosquitos were feeding on me as easy prey, and it was becoming unpleasant out here so exposed. My pack was filled with what I could grab from Helen's stuff and should carry me for days if something went wrong. I located the remainder of the diamonds, which was good, because I didn't think the locals would consider anything less. I just needed to be careful and not play into anyone's greed or for sure, a bullet in the head would be the final negotiation. Hell, I don't even know what the Colombians used for cash or what they called it. I bet Helen could tell me in a second as well as what denominations.

I needed to keep the words of Helen in mind: "The city of Buenaventura has a reputation for being one of Colombia's highest crime cities, so we have to be vigilant!" Considering my Idaho urban skills in handling dangerous situations were zero, I was sure to be tested. Right then, I felt almost as if on autopilot. I could just take the diamonds, make a run for it, and hope to elude world capture. However, with what I had inside my head, there wasn't any way I could avoid capture down the road. For now, I had to assume that I was the number one fugitive on this planet. Considering the implications of finishing this mission—world dictators, governments, wars, and genocide would all come to a sudden halt. What would a world of people growing with a sense of empathy for each other be like? Sure, initially the infrastructure would collapse, but think hundreds of years into the future, how children of multiple generations would revitalize our civilization and focus their energy on positive things rather than destructive elements.

Ahhh…that was the ocean off to my right I was hearing. I needed to get out of the jungle; I had enough bug bites and cuts on my hands that if not treated, I would probably get an infection in a few days. Great, I view a clearing just up ahead and sand, which was a promising site. What a relief. I was starting to get claustrophobic that I might be on the wrong directional path and doomed in the jungle.

Pulling the last jungle branch aside and looking out over the bay, I fell to my knees and elated in the sight of the coastline. Awesome, I wished Helen were by my side. A wave of loneliness swept over me, even though I had made it this far. Helen had painted a picture that we would eventually reach the ocean bay. However, the best way would be a boat ride across the bay, which was around eight to ten miles. If I hugged the coast, it would be quite a walk that would probably wear me down beyond my supplies. A quick boat ride was the best solution since plenty of fishermen would probably take a few diamonds for passage.

Walking along, it looked like a pillar of smoke rising around the bend. Maybe someone could be my source for transportation. Taking Helen's thinking in mind, I should approach from a hidden position in the jungle and look around before jumping into a conversation. In addition, that should give me some time to figure out how to communicate getting to the city with my few words of Spanish. Hindsight being 20:20, I should have had Helen coaching me. Entering the jungle gave me apprehension, but the only way to make this work was to be methodical, in the footsteps of Helen. I could view a few huts, the normal barking dog, and fish drying on racks. Yes, there was a boat with an outboard motor that should be able to handle the excursion I had in mind. Since the boats looked old and beaten, I would guess they were not purchased through the drug trade, which was a positive note.

Slowly working my way towards the huts, I decided I shouldn't sneak up but should be out in the open. That would position me as a less threatening element in my approach. How would I explain to anyone ending up on this obscure beach alone and looking as out of place as one could imagine? I wasn't sure if portraying a lost tourist from a posh resort in the area would work since I had no idea what was around this place.

"Gringo, que pasa?" asked a smallish man as he approached from the hut.

"No hablo Español," I said to communicate, not being able to speak Spanish.

The guy looking at me was just as perplexed as I was at this moment. I could smell his lack of daily bathing and the grime and sweat of living in the jungle. His clothes, tattered and smelling of fish, were a good sign he was most likely the owner of the boat.

He smiled at me, raised his arms in the air, and started laughing, which was a good sign he wasn't going to pull out a gun and shoot me. I smiled back and pointed to myself: "Muy pendejo gringo."

He got my point that I was just stupid and gave me a thumbs up!

All right, professor meets local fisherman—now how to communicate my needs? Well, back to the true and proven method; pictures should work for him. Let's see if a sand drawing would be worthy to get me to the city. I picked up a stick and pointed towards the sand in order to portray there was no threat from me. I created from my mind what would be the bay and a city of my destination. I looked at him for acknowledgement. He got that much. He smiled and said, "Si, si, no problema!"

Good, okay, adding a boat, and directional arrows should be enough to get the point across, which I sketched out on the sand with my limited artistic ability and conceptualization. Then I pointed towards his boat, made a wave for the ocean, and pointed in the direction I wanted to go. I think he got it, since immediately he said, "Si' mi Amigo." Good, we were making progress now; the tough part was how to get in a position of his goodwill. Immediately, once he got the point, he rubbed his fingers together with the universal sign for money, and I smiled back. Helen would be proud of me making it this far, although she probably would have accomplished the same in five minutes versus me going on thirty.

Now the tough part, conversion of diamonds to what it's worth for a boat ride across the bay. I didn't want to be two forward or easy for this guy to roll over. I jumbled through the backpack intently, made a lot of noise, finally placed the pack on the ground, and opened the small stash of diamonds. I pulled out one that looked fitting and at least 1.5 carats; it should be worth several thousand dollars.

"Señor, this should cover my passage," I said, passing the diamond over.

The fisherman looked at me and took the diamond out of my hands and examined it then held it up to the sky. Not sure how many local fishermen were diamond experts, but shortly he said, "Si, Vamanos."

I observed as he waved in the air, motioning to another man. "Jose vamos, rapido."

The man approached the edge of the beach. He was dressed in tattered clothes, no shoes, and a wide-brim cowboy hat that looked aged. Gosh, I sure hoped this guy wasn't bad news, although I now could view his holstered machete. Whatever they were plotting, hopefully didn't include dumping me in the ocean and grabbing the stash of diamonds.

I had better take the upper hand. "Hombres, vamos ahora," I said as I pointed to the horizon. Both men looked at me and then exchanged a few more words. Jose gave me a thumbs up and a smile with half his teeth missing. They motioned to me to get into the boat, and then I contemplated my safety was less if both men were in the boat. Most likely, they would plot something together. Once in the boat, I rose and motioned sternly; only one person in the boat was coming along as I glared my eyes at both of them and dug my hand into the pack. I hoped that they thought that I held a gun in reserve, which of course wasn't true. They both stood in silence while looking at me; then Jose handed the rope over to the lone fisherman. He motioned with his fingers the need for more cash.

At that point, I agreed, but motioned that once we arrived at the city, I would give him another diamond. He motioned with two fingers his needs. No way, I motioned back; one finger and that's it with a hand wave. He looked over to Jose and acknowledged that the negotiation was over.

Whew, that was a close call. I had no idea what these two had in mind, but the outcome with the two of them onboard could go ugly halfway across the bay. I felt a lot more at ease knowing if things went bad I only had one person to deal with. Jose helped push the two of us off, the outboard motor quickly started, and the fisherman turned the boat southeast, which was a good sign all was well. It was nice to be back on the ocean and away from the hot jungle with bugs and unknown factors. This was sort of like my final goodbye to Helen, since even if I returned to this spot; there was little chance in the chaos of the jungle that I would ever find her body.

With the waves bouncing against the boat and the sound of the loud outboard motor, I found some final peace and time to think. Once I got to the city, since I was cash poor, I needed to find some way to get my hands on local currency. My best option was to find a jeweler that might speak English and was willing to exchange diamonds for local currency. Yes, that is what I needed to do quickly. Then I would find a cheap hotel room, get some rest, and plot my next move. There was no way I could go any farther without renewed energy and some decent food. I really felt alone looking over the vast ocean and thinking of Helen left behind...

CHAPTER 18 ♈ JOURNEY UPHILL

Luckily, there were no issues getting across the bay with my local boat transport even though one eye was kept off to the side to gain a better idea of whether my transportation planned to make a move. A quick hit would be all it would take, and then he could toss me over the side for shark bait. Maybe there was his fear of reprisal not knowing who I was or where I came from. Then again, maybe he was a good person and didn't wish to hack me to pieces. The shore approach provided a good view of the city relative to the perspective from the boat as it hopped across the wave.

The beach looked nonexistent, as this was a coastal town with boat docks and heavy overhead cranes. For better or worse, it should be a good starting point for making some connections. It was just a question of how in the world I would make any progress without Helen. Approaching the dock, the boat was maneuvered to allow better access and tied up to at least allow me an easy exit. Once on the dock, I opened up the diamond bag and handed one more to the boatman. I wasn't sure if that was the end of our deal, but he gave me a slight head nod as acknowledgement. It was probably time to get out of here before he found any friends to finish me off. I couldn't be too sure if he was a friend, foe, or executioner.

I first need to figure out how to get some local cash and make a trade for diamonds without attracting too much attention. Okay, now what would I do in a crowded airport when needing directions? Hmmm…looking for a good-looking girl and playing stupid tourist always works. It looked like a small group of local girls congregating near what appeared to be a small restaurant. I just needed to build up some confidence to pull this off and not come off sounding too stupid.

"Hola, senoritas. Habla English?" I said with some hesitation. Gosh, I hoped that did the trick because those were the few words I could remember. All three girls looked at me and smiled, but only one girl with long black hair and extra thick eyebrows spoke up in broken but understandable English.

"Yes, I speak English. But just a little bit," she said. I reached out to introduce myself but thought best to use the long form of my name.

"Hello, my name is William."

"Hello, William. My name is Adelina," she said along with a gentle handshake.

Well, that was easy enough, and it never hurts to provide smiles and a happy-looking face, although I must have looked like a tattered mess after the jungle excursion, with no shower and dirt and grime on my face.

"Thank you for talking to me. I'm in need of some help," I said, not knowing what would sound reasonable with this girl.

"You look like a big mess," Adelina said with a sarcastic smile. She was well dressed in nice slacks and what appeared to be reasonable jewelry to reflect on her social status in life.

"Yes, I'm a mess, and you wouldn't believe what I've gone through in the last several days."

The other two girls both looked at me with deep suspicion as the three of them chatted in Spanish with no consideration to the fact that I was standing next to them. One of the girls raised her hands in a motion that indicated I was a questionable character. Nevertheless, Adelina shook her head, which hopefully meant she was siding with me.

"William, my two friends need to be going. I will sit with you and listen to your story," Adelina said with sincerity.

Wow, what a stroke of great luck! I had just landed on the coast, and a perfect stranger was willing to help me out. That was a great sign of the empathy

Helen spoke of—people helping others without a consideration of the consequences. I was sure Helen would be thinking, Duh, I think Liam finally got it. A feeling of well-being swept over me; I think this is what the world is supposed to be like.

"Gosh, that would be fantastic!" I said in return.

Adelina directed us to a small outdoor place where we could sit and have a drink that was around the corner. Truthfully, sitting having a drink was the best thing right now, but having no cash was a big problem. It was time to take a big gamble. I needed to sit with her and offer her a diamond. That should do the trick. Approaching the location, I could view a quaint place with five tables with chairs, all empty at this time of the day. It was a good idea to sit outside just in case I needed to make a quick exit if things went south with Adelina too quickly. I needed to remember Helen's words that this town was not user friendly and had a high level of criminal activity. Adelina could just be baiting me and then make a move to gain an upper hand. It was best to remain paranoid.

Sitting, Adelina waved down the waiter. "William, what would you like to drink?"

"Ahhh…whatever you are having would be great," I said with some hesitation.

"Okay, hopefully our local beer works for you," Adelina said as I smiled back with approval.

"Senor, Dos Club Colombia Roja, por favor," said Adelina to the waiter.

Beer I liked this girl already, and that was the last thing I would have expected. Cold, warm, or whatever, a beer worked for me.

"So, William, what brings you to Buenaventura?" asked Adelina.

Gosh, I knew that question would eventually surface. I needed to think of a reasonable story to provide to her. Telling Adelina I was on a mission to alter the fate of humanity would probably not go over very well. But then again, maybe she was a person of empathy that Helen spoke of and is in the small percentage of the population that would transcend evolution. What would Helen do? That was a good question and a decision in the next few minutes that might change my destiny.

"Well, to be truthful, I'm on a mission to save someone, and time is running out," I said, contemplating how that would go over.

"Okay, so is this a friend or a lover?" asked Adelina.

"Well, I guess you could say a very good friend that is dear to my heart."

"William, what happens if you don't succeed?"

"Well, sadly, I'm not sure considering the way the world is currently in turmoil," I said.

"You mean the tragic nuclear explosions that have upset the balance of countries, governments, and financial markets?" said Adelina with a hint of trauma.

"Yes, in a way, those events are meant to create chaos, but in turn, they may be the beginning of worse things to come," I said.

I watched a glimmer from Adelina as if there was something deep in this girl and that a hip outfit and upscale look of sophistication was just her facade.

"William, my father said last night to me on the phone, Adelina, the world is about to take a turn for the worst. Our lives may never be the same."

"Adelina, I'm afraid he may be right, and I can sense something in your heart you want to help me because of that possibility," I said, taking a huge chance this was a woman who would survive with the release of the virus. I could envision this girl taking a leadership role to pull together people after the passing. There was something in her that stood out.

"William, as you noticed, my friends weren't very fond of you, and that is why they left," said Adelina with a tight lip.

"Yes, I sort of sensed that's what happened."

"But they know me for being sort of the weird person out to help people in spite of the odds of success. So they left and were rude about it."

"I'm sorry to hear that, but I will tell you one thing. That trait you have will change the world someday—so don't lose it," I said with a smile on my face.

"Well, I sure hope so because my father has protected me and always has one watchful eye on me," said Adelina.

"Hey, that is what fathers do and especially to kind and thoughtful daughters," I said with sincerity.

I could tell from our discussion that Adelina was breaching a chasm of differences between us. This exchange rather sounded like the picture Helen had painted in my mind. People would eventually learn to live together, not apart and indifferent, with an overshadowing sense of empathy. It was like a breath of relief at this moment, almost as if Helen sent me a guardian angel just at the right time!

"Yes, and considering the many dangers in Colombia and especially for a gringo such as yourself, you won't get many chances in this country to survive if you make a wrong turn!" exclaimed Adelina.

"I fully understand and have to consider my next move. I need to convert some stones to cash and get a hotel or something to recover from the last several days," I said, hoping Adelina got the idea of stones.

"Stones, you mean diamonds—are they blood diamonds?" asked Adelina.

Heck, I hadn't any idea where Helen got the diamonds, but I was sure she didn't dig them up herself. I would expect she collected them over time, so as not to draw suspicion.

"No, what I have isn't blood diamonds, but they were provided by a very kind woman, much like yourself. Unfortunately, she has passed away, so I'm left with this personal dilemma of dealing with the diamonds," I said.

"Okay, I don't want to pry too much, but once you exchange those diamonds for cash, you will need to move fast because the news of you will hit the streets very quickly."

"Yes, that makes sense, and it's something I didn't think about," I said with a grin.

"Okay, no more said. You are coming home with me. I will call my parents and tell them we have a distressed foreigner from a charity organization. They usually have compassion for people who help our country."

"Are you serious? That isn't quite what I expected," I said with disbelief.

"I do this for you, and in some way a good favor will be returned in life for me some day," said Adelina.

Helen reflected on a world where the minds of indifference would be filled with the few that carried the DNA of empathy. Self-centered individuals wouldn't be part of the equation to allow evolution of people to grow, change, and evolve. I truly felt vulnerable right now and had nowhere or no one to turn to, so this was my only option.

"I fully understand your thinking, and I'm in your hands," I said with sincerity to Adelina.

As I walked along the streets with Adelina, I felt a lot more relaxed with her. There was no way I would have been able to navigate the streets alone. A few people appeared to recognize her and provided cordial expressions, almost as if she was a princess and not to be messed with. I found that rather strange, but maybe it was some cultural nuance I just didn't understand. On my behalf, I must have presented more of the derelict since my clothes were stained with sweat and torn in many places after running through the jungle. I noted the blood stains on my sleeve from

Helen's dying in my arms. I couldn't let sadness overwhelm my heart right now. My head was telling me Adelina is genuine, but my logic was saying keep the defenses up since this might just be a trap to finish me off.

"Here we go. This is my home," Adelina said as she pointed to this gated home with high walls and spikes at the top. How her parents managed this type of wealth here in Colombia, I wasn't about to question and just hoped it was all on good merits.

"Wow, this is a very nice place!" I said with admiration.

"Yes, my parents have some local investments that have changed our lives."

Adelina escorted me past the two-armed guards at the gate and Rottweiler dogs that carefully sniffed us as we passed near them. I had never visited a home with armed guards and vicious dogs that would tear my heart out with one command from their masters. I can't say it was a comfortable feeling entering the compound. Inside the home, Adelina spoke in Spanish to the housekeepers, who quickly mobilized to accommodate me.

"William, we are first going to get you freshened up and maybe get you a light snack and some rest. Then we can talk over a few things that might be on your mind. How does that sound?" asked Adelina.

"That would be grand, and muchas gracias," I said in solemn appreciation.

Later that afternoon…

Ahhh that must be Adelina knocking.

"Hello, William. You look much better and refreshed," said Adelina.

"Yes and it's amazing what a good shower and a nap did for my well-being," I said with sincere satisfaction.

"William, we need to talk. Something bad has happened in the world," said Adelina.

"Please sit down," I said, motioning to Adelina.

Adelina's state of confusion was clear, and that didn't make me feel very comfortable.

"William, just an hour ago, a third nuclear weapon was detonated on Chengjiao Dao Island near the eastern coast of China," said Adelina with an unsteady voice.

"Are you serious?" I said knowing worldly events were escalating.

"Yes and the Chinese mainland is in trouble, with fall-out from the trade-winds believed to be heading towards their coast," said Adelina.

This was very serious now that three nuclear weapons on Chinese, Russian, and American soil had been detonated. Helen had eluded that the time would come when the powers to be would engage in additional chaos that could lead to world collapse. The beginning of some type of power positioning to control the world was in play. Was this the last straw that would create the chaos factor for our de-evolution into more hatred, wars, and economic collapse? Not all of this made sense, but it was becoming a reality I couldn't ignore. In the past few days, I had considered backing out and finding my way back home. However, as Helen mentioned, most likely I would be a dead man in the eyes of the evil behind all of this. Good or bad, the only freedom from all of this was forward motion to end the mission.

"It has gotten very bad, with massive riots all over the world. Banks are being looted, grocery stores emptied, and killings in most major cities. I'm afraid more than ever for my family, who are away on business in Europe," said Adelina, very close to tears.

I knew modesty should prevail and leaned over as a friend to Adelina to comfort her. Here was a young woman who had more than just empathy in her heart but caring thoughts for family and those around her. Now I fully understood what Helen had communicated as the essence of human evolution. I could feel the spirit in front of me and what this would bring to the world where an entire population of people like Adelina would inherit the planet. They would change the world, and they would give rise to our ability to live together, work together, and grow together. This was the evolution that rested in my hands.

"Thank you, William. I know we just met, but in my soul, I know you're a kind man. Maybe lost, but still a nice person with a good heart," said Adelina, wiping a few tears from her face.

"Well, I hope so because I may need you to save my life," I said, attempting not to give too much confidential information away. There was still a sense of insecurity that Helen had drilled in me to never lose sight of paranoia in completing the mission. There was no way at this point I would consider divulging my final location. No one must learn the mission's end or all would be lost.

"William, are you in trouble?" asked Adelina as she leaned away.

"Well, not in a bad way or running from the police. What I need is to figure out how to get from here to Peru in the most expedient manner but not through normal transportation avenues," I said, knowing upfront that it had to make very little sense to her.

"So you need to be sneaky, is what you are telling me?"

"Yes, and I have no idea what to do. But I do have the means to pay for transportation."

"Okay, now we are getting somewhere. What you need is some very expensive private transportation," said Adelina.

Good, I think our minds were finally starting to connect, and this girl of means may just have an answer for me.

"William, as you probably noticed, my family comes from wealth. How they got it I'm not at liberty to discuss, but they have connections that we may be able to use."

Okay, now I needed to feel this one out—how to get from point A to B without giving the farm away? My best chance to hit Machu Picchu was from Cusco from my limited understanding of world geography. What I really needed to do is get on the internet but avoid any tracking of my whereabouts.

"Adelina, I'm going to be upfront with you. I need a plane to get to Cusco."

"Well, that can be arranged. We have a small airport, Gerardo Tobar Lopez, where many turboprop planes land daily. The other option is to fly out of Bogota."

"If I could avoid Bogota that would probably be a good idea," I said, knowing multiple airport connections could trip me up.

"The problem is most of the small turbo prop planes are only good for around 1000 kilometers, and a straight shot to Cusco would be impossible. You may need at least a few airport stops to refuel."

"That's not good news for sure, since that would take some coordination," I said, contemplating the logistics.

"Yes, it would take some doing, but we would need to leave that to the pilot to figure out. Thus the reason for an expensive flight for you and me," said Adelina with a wince.

Wait—where did the "we" come into this equation? There was no way I would ever get Adelina involved in this mission. I would be putting her life in danger and couldn't consider her as collateral under any situation. I best keep things quiet with her and just play along. At some point in time, I needed to give her a push-off but not until further down the path when all arrangements were made. I knew she would probably be very upset, but that was all I could think of as an option right now.

As I raised my eyebrows and looked at Adelina, I said, "Yes, we need the entire plane to ourselves."

Adelina smiled. "William, somehow I feel like your guardian angel and like we were meant to meet."

"No doubt, you are my guardian angel, and life has a way of bringing good people together," I said, contemplating the good and bad of what I had done prior—the boat sinking and what I was tasked with in the very near future that would touch every life on this planet. Helen found me for a reason, and now I had to be brave and confident to pull this off. She had told me the meek shall inherit the earth, and I sure hoped that Adelina was included since she was surely a good person.

"Okay, William, get some rest, and dinner will be served in an hour. I need to see if I can connect with my parents on the internet. I'm going to keep our project quiet. No need to flip them out," she said with a friendly smile.

"Thanks...I think that is a wise decision," I said, contemplating what global network was currently searching for my whereabouts and my ulterior motives.

Later that evening…

"I hope you don't mind sandwiches in the kitchen. I can't say much for my cooking abilities, and the maids have left for the day."

"Works for me, and considering what I have endured the last few days, that sounds like a feast," I said, finally considering a decent meal after several days of backpack food.

"William, I don't mean to pry, but my curiosity does elude me in understanding you. Is it something we can talk about?"

Looking over at Adelina, I knew in my mind there was a fine line between telling the truth and maintaining her support. It was probably best to skew the truth, hopefully for her acceptance.

"Well, Adelina, I'm on a very lonely mission—nothing illegal or what I would call bad, but necessary."

"So are you being chased or have something that belongs to someone else?" asked Adelina.

I needed to be careful in my response—she was digging now. "I don't think anyone is trailing me, and I have nothing in terms of something anyone would want." Well, that should hold her for a few minutes, and to some degree, it was true since who knows if I was being tracked or not.

"I'm on a mission that isn't governmental, political, or, for that matter, an act of terrorism. I guess you could call it more of a mission of the heart and soul," I said, thinking it was time to taper off this line of questioning.

"Okay, I think you have me totally confused. You can't tell me the truth for my own well-being?"

"You're right. The less I tell you, the better off you are," I said knowing that was the truth.

Adelina looked over to me. "While you were resting, I called my friend Fernando, whose father is a pilot for a local business. Please don't ask me what business, because just like your story, I can't provide more than that," said Adelina with a raised eyebrow.

Hmmm…got it for sure; I could only imagine what kind of business either her friend, parents, or associates would be in here in Colombia.

"I fully understand the privacy of asking too many questions. So what's next?" I asked.

"Tomorrow at 10 a.m. we will meet Fernando and his father at a small coffee cafe to talk."

"That sounds great!"

"Well, don't get too excited yet. We have to consider what you have to offer for the transportation to Cusco before we meet up with them," Adelina said with a serious look.

"Adelina, I have that 100% covered and should be able to provide payment."

"Great, I was a little worried about that because this isn't going to be a coach class ticket with these guys. It will be expensive for an illegal flight to Cusco, but it can be arranged," said Adelina with hesitation.

Whew, I wasn't sure what to expect, but it looked one-step closer to Cusco. I had the diamond bag tied to the inner portion of my pants. There was no way I would leave them out of my possession at any time. They represented my only chance of getting to Cusco.

"Adelina, I sincerely appreciate your help, but let's change the subject. Did you get a hold of your parents?"

With a solemn look, Adelina spoke. "Yes, they are doing okay. However, with the current global chaos, they are stuck in Europe."

"I'm sorry to hear that. I hope they are at least safe."

"Safe is a relative term these days. I turned off the news because everything is in turmoil in many western countries. Here in Colombia, we are used to chaos, so that is business as usual. People here appear to be less rattled but still cautious," said Adelina.

"Not sure what you mean?" I asked.

"Well, the western countries are rioting, there's looting, and people are being killed. Nevertheless, here in Colombia, we have gone through such turmoil for so many years that our ability to deal with global crises is calmer. I think that is the proper word."

"Yeah, now that makes a lot of sense!"

"Yes, we are calm in the face of the approaching storm," Adelina said.

"You used the word storm—why?"

"I can feel a storm coming, and I don't know what it is. When there is chaos and turmoil in the world, I fear the end is coming, and there is nothing we can do to stop it," said Adelina with a sigh.

Adelina was very perceptive for a young woman. I could see in her eyes a deep connection with thinking through issues. Her sense of empathy was also giving her the outcome of what may prevail in the world over the next several days.

I carried on with "Yes, the world is in trouble. If you think of all the eons we have spent building civilization and cultures, you can see how very delicate it actually is."

"Yes, very delicate and I'm afraid," said Adelina.

"Adelina, I'm also afraid. Nevertheless, let me tell you something. No matter what happens, you have to reflect and not lose your empathy for others—does that make sense?"

"I'm not sure what you mean."

"You have a spirit and mind of empathy and it will be challenged, but it is the key to your survival. That is all I can say, and you just have to trust me on what it means," I said with a troubled smile.

Gosh, this must be how Helen felt speaking with me. The roles had now been reversed, and I was sitting across from myself with questions, concerns, fear, and uncertainty. Not that I could ever live up to Helen, but this conversation provided me with a much better appreciation of what she did to keep me alive.

We finished our light sandwiches and dinner to close the evening. Tomorrow would make or break the next step in the mission.

The next morning…

Walking along with Adelina, I could tell she was nervous, but there wasn't much I could do to change the situation. "Adelina, I need to tell you something," I said.

"What's on your mind?"

"Well, when it comes to payment for the trip to Cusco, I don't have any cash. I only have diamonds I mentioned prior to cover payment," I said.

"Oh well, here in Colombia, diamonds are even better than cash. You should be good. Just be aware that as a gringo there is less opportunity for negotiation. You won't get the local discount," laughed Adelina.

"I was expecting that." I smiled back.

I could only guess how much the small pouch of diamonds was worth. Not being an expert on anything except academic logic and brands of yogurt put me at a real disadvantage. I should have sat down last night and counted them out. My best estimate was at least 200 uncut stones from one to three carats, which should bring a decent price.

"Most likely they will want to see what you have and not just accept your word. Since there will be some good faith involved, you may have to part with a down payment," said Adelina.

"I understand, and we will need to consider how much."

"Yes, and as this is Colombia, someone will catch wind of your situation, so we may need to pay a little hush money at the same time," Iterated Adelina with a grin.

Street smarts—I could say my head was as dull as could be when it came to such negotiations. The last thing I needed was to be gunned down and have all the diamonds stolen. My only hope was that Adelina's association with Fernando was good enough to provide reasonable cooperation without bodily harm.

"Here we are, and there is Fernando and his father," Adelina said approaching the small quaint outdoor café set off from the main street.

Fernando looked in his late teens, which would be fitting with Adelina's friend and his father, a slightly graying man with a healthy disposition in looks. Both were sitting outside; that should give us some privacy, so no one could overhear our conversations.

"Hola, Fernando," said Adelina as she reached down to give him a small hug and cheeky kiss. In turn, Fernando's father got up and gave Adelina a small hug. It was good to see there was a friendly relationship between these three. Adelina conveyed something in Spanish, which I didn't understand, but several smiles transpired, which was encouraging.

"William, please meet Fernando and Senor Sosa." Adelina was politely introducing the three of us, and both of them got up to shake my hand. "We will use as much English as possible, but please be patient with Mr. Sosa and Fernando. I may need to translate to ensure everything is clear."

"Okay, not a problem, and I truly appreciate everyone reaching out to help me," I said, considering if they only knew the depth of my needs and the mission, they would probably hand me over immediately to the authorities. No one would want to be part of a global event like what I have the potential to unleash.

"William, Adelina has told us about your travel request, and I think I have a few options available," said Mr. Sosa.

"Great. I'm all ears." I smiled back, although I wasn't sure if all ears was a term common in South America.

"Yes, I have an associate who can fly in a Bombardier 70 from Bogota to pick you up. Our small airport is tight, but the runaway with this particular jet will allow us 500 feet of takeoff margin. The plane has a 2,060-mile range, and the flight to Cusco is around 1,400 miles, so we have plenty of buffer with this aircraft to arrive safely."

"Wow, you have really done your homework, and I appreciate the details," I said, considering I would have to trust Mr. Sosa. "How long do you think it will take us to get there?"

"Depending on wind speeds, it should be around three hours," said Mr. Sosa with confidence.

"Great, that sounds like a great flight plan," I said with some excitement.

"Now, please realize, we assume this is a one-way trip, and we will need to fly the plane back to Bogota. So the price you pay is for your return, and my associate is asking $50,000 USD," said Mr. Sosa with Fernando providing a terse upper lip, indicating some cut would be flowing back to their pockets.

"Yes, that would be acceptable. Now, for payment, I have diamonds to pay and I hope that is okay."

I wasn't sure that was perfectly stated as Mr. Sosa and Fernando looked at each other and then continued in Spanish, discussing something. I could view a few head nods, which I assumed was a good sign.

"William, we should be able to complete the transaction, but in good faith, we would like to evaluate your diamonds and for you to provide us with a down payment to continue this deal."

Well, from Adelina's prior comments, this was to be expected, and it was best to take up counsel with her prior to handing over any stones. ""Adelina, can I have a private word with you?" I asked while smiling at Mr. Sosa and Fernando.

"Sure, William, let's just go inside."

Walking in the café was actually a nice breather from the tense situation of arranging a stealthy flight to Cusco. Dealing with and handing over the diamonds just wasn't in my comfort zone.

"What's up?" asked Adelina as she found a quiet spot for us to talk.

"Well, are you and your friends good with making all of this happen?"

"William, I have known the Sosa family my entire life, and they are good with the arrangements. I know this is scary, but this is the best I can do for you."

"Yeah, I understand, Adelina, and my appreciation is very sincere," I said, considering Adelina was correct. Where in the world could I expect to have such help fall out of the sky? If fate was in the cards, and if my path was sound, this was my ride to Cusco.

"I would recommend you show them the stones, and then they will decide what to take with them. I don't think there is any room for negotiation in this plan," said Adelina.

"Yes, I understand, and we need to get back."

"Yes, best we don't keep them waiting," Adelina said with apprehension.

"Mr. Sosa, I agree to the terms and in good faith will provide a down payment as requested," I said. Slowly, I pulled out the diamond bag, still apprehensive at the thought that this was all I had between life and death in this country. Slowly, I leaned over to Mr. Sosa to look inside the pouch and noted both of his eyebrows rise in admiration.

"These look like good diamonds, and you appear to have enough to cover the deal. I would suggest we take ten diamonds with us to review the quality and value for my associate," said Mr. Sosa.

"Acceptable," I said and started the task of randomly picking out ten diamonds to hand over to Mr. Sosa. He remained silent in anticipation of the diamonds being handed over to him. As I provided ten diamonds, I observed Mr. Sosa providing a slight smile. He must have appreciated the merchandise in spite of my understanding of what they were truly worth. It's not as if I would know if I was being taken advantage of at this moment.

"Well, William, these are very nice stones, and I'm sure we shouldn't have any problems getting your plane ride in order," said Mr. Sosa while smiling at Fernando. "It will probably take us a few days to make the arrangements, so I recommend you lay low until then. I will contact Adelina when it is time for you to be at the airport."

"Okay, that sounds good," I said.

"Also, expect to hand over at least fifty of those stones, and that should close the deal. Can you do that?"

"Yes, I got it covered."

"Also, please note there is an extreme penalty for not showing at the airstrip, and Colombians don't take kindly to being crossed. I hope that doesn't sound too stern, but once the arrangements have been made, you have no choice but to close the deal," said Mr. Sosa with a very deep look of seriousness.

I could fully appreciate what Mr. Sosa was conveying: no show and someone would be coming for the diamonds and me. There was no way I would survive the local street gangs, and I needed to consider Adelina's safety, not just mine.

"Mr. Sosa, I appreciate your assistance, and I'm good to go." I shook hands to close the deal with Mr. Sosa and Fernando. There was only the need to figure out how to get from Cusco to Machu Picchu and trigger the event. I couldn't even fathom that moment. It's almost like a distant movie script that I shouldn't even be involved in.

Adelina spoke in Spanish to Mr. Sosa and Fernando with a hug and smiles as they departed. Gosh, I just wished Helen were here; I felt so stupid trusting these strangers with my future. My only hope was that Adelina would be true to her word.

CHAPTER 19 ⚼ TRUTH OR TRUST

I could truly say that yesterday was more than stressful—it was way out of my comfort zone. I felt like a Boy Scout graduating to Eagle level after the last several days. I needed to get the mission in my head squared away. I also need to get my hands on some Peruvian money, and for that, hopefully Adelina could help. Once I get to Cusco, I need to figure out how to meander to Machu Picchu. I'm sure a quick internet search would settle that one. In the town of Cusco, I would need to avoid relaxing, rise to the occasion, and get the flip out of there as quickly as possible. Must be vigilant someone may be tracking me. Maybe my stupidity and naïve nature were keeping them off track since my efforts were chaotic and random more than logical.

Ahhh…thinking of Helen the first day I met her and not knowing what would transpire. There she sat as I provided my viewpoint on burning down all the forest, and her missing the point of the assignment. Little did I realize the message she was providing was foreshadowing. Gosh, it was just like yesterday sitting in the small café in Moscow, Idaho, with Helen next to me. The beauty and warmth she projected into my heart was like nothing I had ever felt before. The ragged basement she lived in, but content in the isolation it allowed her. Okay, so she kidnapped me and carted me across the border to Mexico—that was the defining moment for me, and probably it was best to be drugged and unconscious. It was crazy, but it brought a smile to my face just thinking of it. Right now, I can feel her spirited presence is nearby, watching over me.

Knock on the door…

"Good morning. You look refreshed and ready to roll," said Adelina.

"Well, not sure if I'm ready to roll, but what a difference a good night's rest made for me. I can tell you, without your generosity, I'm not sure I would have survived a few more days," I said with a smile.

"You did look a little ragged when I first met you."

Ragged, torn, confused, dazed, all the above—if I considered sinking a ship, meandering through a jungle, and making it to this city without Helen. I could still see her face looking up at me just before I covered it with the remaining palm trees and debris. For sure, she was my hero left behind but never to be forgotten. Now it was up to me to finish this for her.

"William, I did hear from Mr. Sosa, and he was very positive that everything is moving forward. He also confirmed the ten diamonds were good quality and covered his payment for arranging the deal. But we need to go over a few details."

"Sure."

"Well first, as you know, not all business in Colombia is, how can I say...legitimate," said Adelina with a grin, "...and it's best to just make the exchange and ask no questions. That includes even eye contact."

Good that I had training on the drug ship since Helen kept me at bay when it came to interactions with the crew. Most of them could have probably snapped my neck or put a round in me without even giving it a second thought. It is amazing how one minute all is normal and then it transcends into chaos and life threatening fear. I always felt on the ship that just one wrong word or gesture could lead to my demise.

"Makes perfect sense to me," I said with sincerity.

"One more thing. Same with my parents—they are off limits for any questions. Where our money comes from is something no one talks about since it can lead down paths that are best left untouched," said Adelina with a stiff upper lip.

"I understand, Adelina, and I appreciate you being upfront with me!"

"Now, today we have a few things to tidy up. I expect by noon to hear back from Mr. Sosa, and if all is good, we will need to move fast. As you requested, this will be a stealthy run to Cusco, and your presence, name, and any other information will be kept confidential. You can say the diamonds bought you secrecy."

"Makes sense to me—I do have a few questions though," I said.

"Sure, go ahead," said Adelina.

"Well, I think we need to have some local Peruvian money for the trip and maybe some light food for our packs."

Using these words hopefully settled well with Adelina. I had no plans to bring her any farther than the airport, but I couldn't let on. In her mind, she thought this was more of an adventure than a mission and a one-way trip. Of course, I didn't want her to know about the next leg of the trip from Cusco, since the end destination would potentially be the most treacherous for the excursion.

"Not to worry. I can take care of money for us, and if you don't mind, I will need a few of the diamonds for an exchange. As for food, our pantry is filled with goodies, and we can take whatever we need. My parents are like food pack-rats—always prepared for a siege or the end of the world," Adelina said with a sarcastic laugh.

"Adelina, I would prefer if you would take a few of the diamonds for yourself. If that is okay," I said.

This girl was going way beyond amazing to help me out. I didn't really know how I could ever repay her for this debt of gratitude.

"William, can I be truthful with you?"

"Sure."

"My parents would freak out if they knew what I'm doing to assist you. The house help I'm sure will tell them or have already told them, and I'm already walking a thin line here. I just need to do this, so don't worry about the diamonds for me. You need them," Adelina said with sincerity.

"Adelina, you are truly a dear and a wonderful person with a great heart."

"Well, if we get to Cusco, then we can discuss that to a further length. I would suggest you stay put in your room, and I will take a couple of diamonds to get us Peruvian sol from the street money changer," said Adelina.

"That sounds great, and truthfully, I could really use additional down time before we depart," I said, considering I had no idea when I would again feel the comforts of a beautiful home and soft bed. When the world collapsed to a smaller population, this could be my last good night sleep. Deciding not to ponder the outcome, I focused on the mission set before me. I had zero thought of backing out. If my last breath was pushing bumps on some rock somewhere in Machu Picchu, it had to be done.

"One more thing, William. We have satellite television, and a few broadcasts are in English.

The news isn't good, so be prepared for a world in complete turmoil," Adelina said with concern.

"Adelina, have you heard from your parents since yesterday?"

"I haven't, and I just hope they're okay," she said with a sadness in her voice. I wasn't sure what else I could communicate to comfort her. She may never see her parents again, or her life could end. Although, Adelina is an inspiration of hope and empathy for what this world needs. If the meek shall inherit the world, I hoped she was on the list of those that would survive. I had no concern for my own life or survival.

"I'm sure they are fine and are just holding out to come home," I said with my best attempt at comforting her.

"Yes, I sure hope so. Hey, diamonds and I'm off!"

I rummaged through my little bag of diamonds and spotted a couple that should do the trick for at least an equivalent of several thousand dollars of U.S. currency. Not knowing when I could ever be near another opportunity to exchange diamonds, this was probably my best shot. I just needed enough to survive a few more days, and then this should all be over. Currencies would probably collapse overnight anyway, and who knew what people would barter with across the world.

Adelina scurried off. I needed to get some rest and see what was happening in the world. Finding the remote in Spanish, I guessed the button for "on" was green. There we go, and up and down arrows should be volume and channels. The flat screen television in this room was very upscale, just like the rest of the house. Let's see soap operas, soccer, fashion shows, not much. Wait, this looked like a local news channel I could watch.

Turning my attention to the news channel, my first impressions after several minutes of watching things weren't too good out there. It appeared the turmoil had penetrated all aspects of life, from politics to people to banks. Even though the nukes were somewhat isolated from primary populations, the effect was taking an ugly turn. World disruption was upon us, and no way could the clock be turned back. The intention was to incite riots, create conflict, and disrupt governments. Ultimately, would this be enough to topple humankind on a path of de-evolution. As Helen had stated, things were moving faster than anticipated, and it was now or never, or the chaos would ensue further. The last thing we needed was the release of the nukes by major holders, and it would be all over. I had recently read that there were still around 4,000 active warheads and 16,000 in retention. Letting loose even a small portion of the nukes between the major nations would be non-recoverable for the planet with radiation fallout. Then some control freak dictator would take over the world and begin the steady exploitation into an oppressive government state. Yes, that would be just enough to tip us over the edge, and then consider the chaos, killing, plundering, and suffering everyone would be doomed to endure. Helen knew the end was near, and being hunted was most likely some world regime that didn't want a solution but instead a cruel and unjust world. Empathy would be dead and forever lost if the viral nature of humans was left unabated. I hoped I could give my life to stop such a deplorable world, future and fate of humankind.

Watching the world news flip from one continent to another, it was obvious that the clock was ticking. I needed to finish this…period!

Later that afternoon…

"Liam, Liam wake up…it's me, Helen. We're almost there, and the trackers are nearby. I can't make it any farther, and the rest are stalking us here in the jungle. Please don't think I let you down…."

Whoa…what the heck…whew, that felt so real. I knew it was just a dream, but it was as if Helen was next to me, and I could feel her presence. Trackers, I had not heard that word before. Maybe Helen had mentioned it, but I had forgotten. Whatever, they were out there, and maybe she was reaching out from somewhere to warn me. I didn't think Adelina was on the hook for any bad conspiracy theories today. I still felt she was being quite sincere in her actions, although I really had no idea. I just needed to play it out and get on that flipping jet!

Ahh...that knock on the door must be Adelina. "Hello, William."

"Just a minute. Need to pants up."

Whoa, what time was it? The last time I looked at a clock, it was late morning.

Opening the door, there stood Adelina with her chipper, let's roll personality. "How are you feeling?"

"Not too bad," I said, "but I'm famished for a bite."

"We can go to the kitchen and fix a sandwich or something. Also, our travel plans have been arranged, and I can fill you in."

"Fabulous! Can't wait to hear!"

Heading down to the kitchen, Adelina took to the task of preparing a couple of turkey sandwiches on Pandebonos cheese bread. She spent at least five minutes raving about the bread, which was homemade by the hired help. I was very appreciative of the narrative and provided my appreciation of such a grand meal. In addition, the Carambola star fruit juice to top off the meal was wonderful.

"So, William, what do you think?"

"Well, I can only say I'm coming back to Colombia!" I said with enthusiasm.

"Muy Bueno, amigo!" Adelina conveyed with a smile. After a pause, she added, "William, we have never talked about what you do in life. Can you share?"

Hmmm...not a good sign. I know that is what most people would ask, but it was not good to drop my guard. I just couldn't allow too much personal information out. Any such connectivity when so close to the end goal could turn out to be deadly for me.

"Adelina, I promise to tell you when we return to Colombia. I will tell you everything," I said in order to derail further questioning.

"Okay, promise?" said Adelina, as if she never expected it to go that far.

"Yes, I will tell you everything when we return to Colombia."

"Okay, let's get down to the plans for tomorrow," said Adelina.

"Tomorrow!" I said with excitement.

"Yes, tomorrow we need to be at the airport at 9 AM sharp. The jet will leave Bogota around 8 AM, and it will take approximately one hour to arrive at Gerardo Tobar López Airport on the outskirts of Buenaventura. The plane will top off fuel at the airport, and we can expect to depart around 10 AM to Cusco," said Adelina.

"That sounds great. How long can we expect the flight to Cusco to be?" I asked.

"We should expect around three hours for the 2,000-kilometer flight, pending no delays and issues."

"Okay, so if it all works out, we can expect to be in Cusco around one-ish?" I asked.

"Yes, that is correct," said Adelina.

All right, that's a great plan. I couldn't see any issues besides the exchange of the diamonds and someone killing me on the plane for the remainder of them. In addition, I needed to think of how to graciously sidestep Adelina to keep her off the plane. I needed to ensure she didn't flame out and take any steps to head for the authorities or I'm toast.

"When we arrive in Cusco, the jet will be pulled into the hangar. From there, we need to scoot out of the airport and avoid immigration or the Policía. Now consider, whatever happens after that is a whole other set of variables," Adelina said.

Well, I couldn't say that it shouldn't be nerve-racking to avoid immigration, but as Adelina mentioned, don't ask questions. I would assume someone had been paid off to look the other way when we arrived.

"William, in this area of the world, persuasion in terms of cash goes a long way. However, you have to be careful because if you are in the wrong place at the wrong time, that may be your last exchange. Does that make sense?"

"Yes, perfect sense, and I have that one etched in my mind!" I said, thinking that the next time a roadblock came up; I had better have a quick hand on the cash.

"Now, in terms of money, we have an equivalent of $10,000 Peruvian sol. I will carry half, and you carry the remainder. That way each of us has a fighting chance of keeping our hands on it if something goes wrong," said Adelina, who for a minute sounded like Helen providing her authoritative direction. It was actually somewhat comforting, but from such a young girl, it made me feel a bit lame in my street wisdom.

"Adelina, can I tell you something?"

"Sure."

"I'm thankful and blessed to have your help, and may the world someday find the same passion that you have," I said with sincerity.

Adelina just smiled and laughed. "Okay, all set, now we just need to lay low, and tomorrow I have a driver who will pick us up at 8 AM," said Adelina.

Thinking forward, once I got to Cusco, I would have to utilize my own wits to figure out how to get to Machu Picchu. I would assume that the bad guys would be after me and already have a bead on my head. What I had in my mind would change the entire future of the planet, and they wanted to either stop or capture me and probably torture the crap out of me.

"Oh, one more thing to consider when we get to Cusco," said Adelina.

"What's that?"

"We can still expect to have tourists since this time of year is the high season. Though the world is in utter turmoil, people with plans most likely are still moving around and about. Travel is starting to slow down, but the isolation of Cusco should provide us some cover," said Adelina.

"That's probably a good thing," I said. Considering that the DNA-targeted virus depended on airborne exposure to a handful of people, in less than a few weeks, it would start a path to alter the face of this planet. Unbeknown to anyone, they would be carrying the virus on planes, trains, and other means across this planet. From what Helen mentioned, once the virus was released, it had no weakness to be countered by the medical knowledge on this planet.

"Well, in a way, that is good for us on our travels to Cusco by avoiding the big cities. Just watching some of the news this morning, I could see that utter turmoil has grasped all the big metropolises with riots and looting, and it appears as if many governments are clamping down with martial law."

"Yes, avoiding the major cities is good, and since we have a direct flight with no refueling, it should provide us great cover to avoid the chaos," said Adelina.

Considering my current plight, I would expect the level of chaos would add some cover if anyone were closing in on my path. If the timing was right and there were no further complications, I could be in Machu Picchu in just a few days. Again, how to get that final few miles was going to be my challenge.

"William, I'm quite worried. The world has never been in this situation with so much chaos. There is even a rumor of unrest starting here in Colombia. Anytime there is a disruption on the planet, it has a tendency to bring out the nasty in people," said Adelina with concern.

"Yes and one bad thing can lead to more, and before it can be controlled, the masses push it over the edge. I'm also concerned that the clock is surely ticking against humans." I said contemplating what Helen believed would transpire.

Adelina looked at me with one raised eyebrow. "William, why did you use the word humans?"

Whoa, good catch by this girl, and she was right. It was probably not the proper word to use in the context of speaking with Adelina. "Well, your perception precedes you, and I probably shouldn't have spoken in that context," I said, apologetic.

"It just conveys doom that is on the way," Adelina stated with a deep concern on her face.

"You know people always say things will get better—well, it does but sometimes not quite like they expect it to," I said.

"I'm still young and hope to live a good life and doom hopefully isn't the future for the world."

"I fully understand, but let me tell you a story of a dear friend who wrote an interesting story," I said, thinking it was probably a great time to derail Adelina's thinking.

"Sure, go ahead."

"Well, the story goes something like this. In many countries, forests are burned to eliminate the underbrush and debris that many times fuels future large-scale fires. In addition, it converts the nutrients from the debris back into the soil. The burn can also destroy weeds that may be out of control on the ground. We call this a controlled burn that can have benefits down the road in a positive way. Maybe that is where the world is heading, and it just needs a good shake up and the good pieces will fall back in place for our future," I said, contemplating the truth behind my words.

"Well, that makes a lot of sense, but consider the weeds we have in our world today includes wars, crime, destruction of the planet, drugs, political thugs, and on and on. It would take a big fire to clean this mess!" Adelina exclaimed.

"Good point. It would take a really big match," I said with a little humor to slow down this thread of discussion. I could almost feel a chill coming over me. The professor of logic is sitting here with a mission that would change the face of the planet. If I told Adelina the truth, that would create a ripple that could end and change my path. I think she would stop me, and I wouldn't blame her since any reasonable person would do the same. As Helen had said, the mission is for the future of the planet and humankind. It is a monumental decision that's left to one obscure professor from Moscow, Idaho. I just hope the logic holds out for me over the next few days.

"Well, fire is probably not the best means, but the concept of do you lose the entire forest or take out a little bit to make it healthier is the question. What do you think?" I asked in an attempt to extract Adelina's thoughts.

"In the eyes of many, it would be a difficult situation, but in reality, it's a decision I'm not sure I could make," she said with a sigh of apprehension.

"Yes, there is always that moment in time when you have to fast forward and make a decision that has implications for everyone. Something bad is going on right now with the nuke explosions placed strategically at locations to antagonize countries and governments. If I'm reading this right, it's all for a reason, but I just can't figure out why."

"Yes, I'm starting to feel the same way, and my friends are sort of lost in a fog about the whole thing. All they think about is shopping and partying. They don't even want to talk about it or consider the implications," said an exasperated Adelina.

"Well, I think most people are in the same mode, hoping it will all go away so we can get back to our normal lives. But in reality, sometimes things swing too far to the left and never come back," I said, believing that Adelina was starting to understand the world's plight.

"All of this really frightens me, and I just don't have a good feeling everything will turn out all right."

"Adelina, I don't have a crystal ball to make a positive prediction, but I have a feeling something wonderful is going to happen that may surprise the world once the wounds are healed," I said with the closest I could think of in terms of philosophy training with a hidden message. It was tough enough sitting here holding back the truth and knowing she would most likely lose family and friends in what was about to transpire. Moreover, there was the scenario of what would happen to my life. Would I survive? As Helen said, she had no idea yes or no. I could die shortly after leaving Machu Picchu and leave a planet of empathy behind. I could survive and then carry with me an endless amount of guilt for what I did. Maybe it would be best; I could do the deed then jump off a cliff. Gosh, I had to stop this crazy thinking.

"Adelina, I had this dear friend that I lost, and I miss her very much. She gave me inspiration to move on, never give up, and do what is best in all circumstances," I said, thinking deeply of Helen.

"My father has sort of the same thinking since he grew up poor in the jungle and clawed his way to where we are today. But along the way, he gave up a piece of his soul to bad things," said Adelina with a look of apprehension about telling me the truth.

"I would ask more, but it's probably not best since this is personal for you."

"Yes, very personal, and in spite of that, we carry some very bad family baggage. Maybe that is part of why when you dropped out of the sky, I was driven to be your safety net and help you out," Adelina said with a smile.

"Hey, without that net, I would most likely be in a real fix, and I owe you a deep debt of gratitude," I said with sincerity.

"Yes, you do, William, but no matter what, in my heart and for some strange reason, I just feel connected with you."

Connectivity—that was a word Helen had mentioned. Something in people-to-people relationships had been lost in our present state. Would a world of empathy result in more connectivity and less need for confrontations, war, greed, and self-indulgence as the alternative? Seriously, if I did nothing, would the world ever get well, change, or evolve to join the galactic society? Truthfully, my logic and studies in philosophy tell me no, it will never happen. All we can expect is more grief and turmoil as the world grows into another billion people added to the planet in several years. I'm not sure if it's a question of right or wrong anymore, but as Helen conveyed to me, few civilizations survive, and a controlled burn is the only hope for ascension.

The next morning...

A driver drove us to the airport, and Adelina was quite clear on getting us there on time, so our provisions were packed and ready to roll. I kept reflecting on the similarities between Helen and Adelina taking command as needed to move things forward. That added reflection walking through the nightmare jungle with one way in and then a complete loss of direction. I remembered several days ago when I was unsure if I could make it out of the jungle alive when I left Helen behind.

"Are you doing okay?" asked Adelina.

"Yes, doing great, just a little apprehension," I said since I had two tasks: leaving Adelina behind and making it to Cusco in one piece.

"You have nothing to worry about. The arrangements were all made under what you would say an umbrella of goodwill to my father. No one will cross him, and that includes me," said Adelina. Cross, now there was a great word that I needed to keep in mind as I told her she wasn't getting on the plane with me.

As we approached the airport, I could view a set of small buildings and a one-propeller plane parked nearby. The runway was bound on all sides by palm trees and jungle, and flying in must be like looking for a Band-Aid surrounded by green all over the place. Clearing the palm trees at the end of the runway looked like life or death. However, the cutback of trees should be enough to get us safely in the air.

As the driver pulled up to the airport curb, he promptly exited the car and addressed Adelina for payment. She thanked him and handed him a tip that elicited a generous smile.

"William, we are going to meet a man named Rael here and bypass all the normal airport stuff. He will take us to the hangar to wait for our ride. He has been instructed not to ask questions and just get us on the plane," said Helen.

"That sounds good. When will I need to pull out the stones for payment?"

"Once you are on board, the pilot will take payment while in the air. No exchange on the ground to avoid any prying eyes or questions," said Adelina with a serious look on her face.

"Yes, that makes perfect sense," I said.

"Señorita Adelina?" said a man as he approached the two of us.

"Si," said Adelina in response.

"Yo soy Rael," said the man, introducing himself.

The two of them carried on for a few minutes, most likely confirming all the arrangements, and then Rael proceeded to guide us around the airport entrance. It was obvious we would be getting the short tour straight to the hangar area. Well, I can only say that diamonds do have their privileges, and I was sure various payoffs must have been made in the background. We proceeded through a gate and met with another man, who provided us with various nods of confirmation that all was going according to plan. We entered the back of a building as he led us through the gate into an empty maintenance area.

"Usted puede esperar aquí en el sofa," said Rael as he pointed to a beat up old sofa next to the wall. I assumed this was where we needed to wait for the jet to arrive.

"Si Señor Rael, gracias," said Adelina in response.

We sat down on the less than comfortable accommodations and waited. Trying my best to stay cool wasn't easy, but I had to do my best under these circumstances.

"William, you okay?" asked Adelina with a kind smile.

"Yeah, still hanging in there," I said with a small bead of sweat running down my forehead.

"Good! Rael will contact the pilot that all is okay and that we have arrived. We will wait here until the pilot lands the plane and tops off the tanks. After that, he will come to the hangar for us, and then we need to promptly board the plane with no delays. Once we get on the plane, the pilot will collect the final payment from us," said Adelina.

Well, one thing I can say, the world of secret communication setting up a plan in this country was very healthy. Although much of it appeared to be word of mouth to reduce a trail of information—it worked very well.

An hour later...

"Señorita, el avión ha llegado y debemos estar listos para partir en 15 minutos," said Rael, addressing Adelina and glancing briefly at me as he walked away.

"We should be ready to depart in around 15 minutes," said Adelina.

Well, the time had come to do my dirty deed and ditch Adelina. Gosh, I sure hope she takes it well.

"Adelina, I need to be straight with you," I said with a hint of remorse.

"William, you have this bad news look on your face."

"Well, I wouldn't call it bad news but rather a consideration for your personal safety."

"Okay, I'm a big girl, give it to me straight," said Adelina with a stern, serious expression.

"Adelina, I can't risk you joining me."

There, I said it, and I felt rotten considering what Adelina had done for me. She had taken me into her home, made all the arrangements, and now I'm dumping her.

Adelina looked at me with a deep reflection and said, "William, will you come back after whatever you have to finish?"

"Adelina, I wish with all my heart I could make you that promise, but just in case I don't, I want to give you something that means a lot to me." I slowly removed a ring that was given to me by my father just before he passed away. He told me, "Go out there and change the world."

"The ring was given to me by my father, who is no longer with me. You saved my life and in turn may have set in motion events that will bring value to this planet. My father always wanted me to live a great life and have a sense of adventure. Instead, up until now, I spent most of my free time in front of a television, hanging out drinking with friends, or spending marginal time with an old girlfriend. This is the first time in my life I have really grown up and faced living more than I could ever imagine," I said, letting the words sink in with Adelina as she looked quietly at me.

As Adelina took the ring, she reached over to me, and I could see tears welling in her eyes. Reaching out to give me a hug, she said, "You go in peace, and please consider, my door is always open for you. I know you have a good heart, and I will pray that you're safe during your travels."

This moment is about life…life…life that is humbled in the turmoil of chaos. This girl, if she represented the future of humans, was why I had to push on. A world that filters out hate, greed, and turmoil and is filled with people of Adelina's empathy would push us to our best as humans.

"Adelina, you have filled my heart with hope, and I can say no more," I said with emotion in my heart.

Wiping away her tears, I almost could tell she knew this was coming with lingering hope still on her mind to join me.

"It's time for you to depart. I will have a word with the pilots before you take off to ensure no funny business and to ensure my family name is remembered. Also, here is the money we had split up, and don't spend it all on tourist stuff!" said Adelina with a teary smile.

"I appreciate that," I said with thoughts of the heart in this young woman.

As the pilot came through the door, Adelina motioned me to leave. Walking out to the plane, I did a quick look. On the tarmac was a beautiful-looking twin jet aircraft. In my lifetime, I hadn't been anywhere near such a plane besides the occasional perusal in magazines. A small set of stairs reached down to the ground, and I could see the pilot waving us forward in a motion to hurry.

"Por favor date prisa," said the pilot with some level of urgency again.

As we neared the plane, Adelina stopped and said, "Goodbye, and I hope someday we meet again."

"We will, I promise," I said and entered the plane with eyes wide open as I saw the leather seats and wood-trimmed décor. This was very upscale compared to what I normally found on coach flights. I saw the pilot bending over to speak with Adelina as she conveyed a series of instructions in Spanish. Gosh, this was it; I was on my way to the end of the mission and leaving behind another wonderful person who touched my life to move me forward. As I looked one more time, Adelina peeked her head inside the plane with a wave goodbye. I smiled and gave her a thumbs up!

Since I had my choice of seats, I decided on a central location in the plane with a seat facing the right hand side of the plane. It was my pet peeve, I guess, to always take the right side of a plane where my personal comfort level resided. A clank rang out as the pilot closed the door and secured it for takeoff.

Walking back to me, he said, "Mr. William, you can store your gear in any of the seats, and please buckle in. Once we get in the air, we can finish our discussion. My co-pilot has been instructed to stay up front, so I will be your only contact during the flight."

"Okay, got it, and thank you," I said as the pilot gave me a quick acknowledgement nod.

I could hear the twin jet engines winding up outside and the slow purr as the rotations came up to speed to move the plane forward to the runway.

The interior lights dimmed for some unknown reason, but it was comforting for my mind. I needed to courage up since this was commitment time, with no turning back. The plane started to roll slowly forward, and small bumps could be felt from the pavement with repairs of cracks and rippled pavement. As we approached the end of the runway, the pilot turned the front wheel to line up for takeoff. Powering up to full throttle, the plane moved slowly forward, gaining speed as the jungle blurred outside the windows. In no time at all, the plane lifted off the runway and easily cleared the trees as it climbed steeply into the air, followed by a slight bump as we hit an air pocket.

The jungle stretched endlessly below me with a few spots of clearing, and buildings faded below. The jet had a nice ascend rate and within minutes had reached what appeared to be our cruising altitude. I was glad the weather was nice since the last thing I needed was turbulence and nausea to add to my already stressed out mind.

The cockpit door opened, and out stepped the pilot. As he approached me, he stood quite stately and professional. I would guess he had flown many high paying passengers on this plane and understood the level of treatment they expected. As for me, he most likely was coming back for the diamonds, as Adelina had mentioned he would.

"Mr. William, how are you doing?"

"Just great and very smooth ride," I said.

"Yes, this plane handles itself well and is very enjoyable to fly," said the captain with a smile.

Okay, let's get down to business. I'm sure if there are no diamonds, it's a quick exit out the door with no parachute, so best to make this quick.

The pilot pulled a small pouch out of his pocket and motioned to me. "There is one diamond in the pouch, and when I return, please add fifty of the same quality and size, and our deal will be complete."

"Okay, no problem. Just give me about 15 minutes and you can return," I said.

"That will be fine," said the pilot as he walked away.

Well, time to pull the pouch and sort through the diamonds to provide the request of like quality. It would only be a guess on my side, but I figured I was handing over 50% of the true worth of the diamonds. I looked over the diamond in the provided pouch and then proceeded to sort through my collection as I counted out fifty pieces and I placed them in the cup holder of the chair. For the sake of the deal, I decided to drop two extra ones into the pouch. This would give at least one diamond for each pilot to take home to grease the deal.

Shortly, I could hear the cockpit door open, and the pilot promptly exited again. "Mr. William, I hope all is well?" he repeated.

"Yes, all is well," I said as I handed him back the little pouch of diamonds.

"Thank you very much. I will assume no issues, and you can just relax for the next several hours until we arrive in Cusco. Around 30 minutes prior to landing, we will return for our final review of instruction to complete our transaction and discuss your departure from the Cusco Airport," said the pilot.

"That sounds great. I'll talk to you in a bit," I said.

The pilot nodded as he walked away. I had better try to relax since the next several hours may be the last time I had such comfort and find myself at 35,000 feet in a plane.

CHAPTER 20 ♈ THE STORM

"We will be landing shortly," said the pilot as he jarred me back to reality. Wow, I didn't realize the gentle hum of the jet engines and plush leather seats could erase the world.

"Yes, that sounds great," I said in return.

"We need to finish a few business items," said the pilot.

"Sure," I said, hoping the diamond exchange was fine for him.

"First, our deal is complete after you depart the plane. We will pull the plane into the hangar, and an airport attendant will usher you out of the gate and past the airport parking lot. Cusco is a small city with many tourists, so you should have no problem blending in. Once the attendant takes you outside, that's it. Don't return, ask questions, turn around, or attempt to communicate with us. Is that understood?"

"Yes, it's not a problem," I said, reflecting again that in spite of the poverty of this region, they had great capabilities moving people incognito across borders. Then again, the universal language of diamonds does provide results.

"One more thing thank you for the token of appreciation," nodded the pilot, referring to the extra diamonds provided to him and the co-pilot. Walking away the pilot appeared to be well versed in illegal protocols.

Looking out the window, I could see El Peru embossed on one of the local hillsides. Wow, what a beautiful site with the mountains in the background and the peaks of snow. There is nothing like the rural countryside blending into the expanse of a city for a perfect view.

As the jet touched down, the pilot eased off and made a gentle forward motion, contacting the runaway. Maybe the extra diamonds included a perfect landing, but for me, I appreciated the care taken on my behalf. Rolling forward, the jet taxied to the end of the runway and veered toward a low, overhanging, open hangar that appeared abandoned with a few planes parked outside. I could see from the windows a single attendant guiding the plane into the open hangar. Shortly, the engine turbines wound down, and this part of the trip was ending.

The pilot exited the cockpit, approached me, and said, "It was my pleasure having you aboard, and welcome to Cusco."

"Thanks, and the trip was very pleasant with an exceptional landing," I said.

"When I open the door, there will be someone to greet you. Please follow them, and they will escort you out of the airport and to the street. He will also flag down a taxi for you if needed."

"Yes, for sure I will need to catch a taxi," I said, anticipating that it was probably best also to find a travel agency.

"I would also advise you to keep things quiet and peaceful by providing a token of appreciation to the ground agent," said the pilot.

"Yes, good idea."

As the pilot cracked the door open, an older man looked inside to get a quick look at me and provided a quick nod and hand motion—time to roll. Collecting my backpack and proceeding to the door, the pilot provided a salute and smile. I did the same and darted out the door. The attendant made very little eye contact as he led me out of the hangar and past a gate with a ready key to unlock it. As we walked in silence, he didn't appear to be concerned with any security, which meant the skids had been well greased. As I looked around, the weather appeared very mild with plenty of tourists and traffic streaming through the streets.

"Señor, I will flag down a taxi for you. They may not speak English, so I can tell them where you would like to be dropped off."

"Thank you. Please tell the taxi driver I would like to be taken to a good travel agent."

"Si, Señor."

"How much should I pay for a taxi?" I asked, anticipating that I would be ripped off anyway. Then again, in several weeks, money may be meaningless.

"Do not pay the taxi driver any more than 20 sol," said the attendant.

"Great, thank you," as I handed the attendant 500 sol casually while I shook his hand. He got the point as he glanced down quickly to acknowledge the amount. As a taxi was being flagged down, several passed before one stopped and quickly pulled to the curb. The driver and attendant exchanged words in Spanish, and then I was flagged to get in the back seat. I waved and thanked the attendant as the taxi pulled away.

Looking around, the city appeared to be colonial with Spanish influences in architecture. At one time, this was the home of the Incas, who built monumental structures that lasted to this day for the entourage of visiting tourists. The driver was very relaxed as he avoided tourists crossing against traffic and diesel buses churning out pollution. Finally, the driver pulled up to the curve with buildings in various states of decline and a variety of graffiti on the adjacent walls.

"Señor, 15 sol, por favor."

I reached down into my pocket, pulled out 50 sol, and figured I might as well include a tip. Handing over the cash to the driver as I departed, he provided a quick nod and pointed to a sign that read Cusco

Travel Agency. Well, I sure hoped they spoke English, which I would suspect with all the tourists running around this place. Walking towards the travel agency, I noted a nice sign with an appealing logo to complement the name. The street was rather empty, with only a few local people wandering the streets. I could feel the thin air in my lungs; it was refreshing but much more extreme than near my normal Moscow, Idaho, home. Home now there was an image that had long passed by me—my comfortable home with all my niceties and electronic toys to keep my mind engaged. Here I was in a foreign country where I was to unleash an event to ensure the future of the human race. Well, might as well head in and see what I could arrange for the next leg of the mission.

As I opened the door, immediately I was greeted with a "Hello."

"Hello, do you speak English?" I said with my fingers crossed.

"Yes, we all do. My name is Elicia."

She reached out to shake my hand, and I, in return, did the same. I would have to be very careful and stealthy since my next move could seal my fate for success.

"Nice to meet you. My name is William," I said, thinking the long form of Liam I used in Colombia would be truthful but provide a curveball for tracking me.

"Well, William, what can we do for you today?" asked Elicia.

"I would like to arrange a trip to Machu Picchu for tomorrow."

"Please sit down, and let me check the train schedule and seats available on my computer," Elicia said as she slowly did a search.

Looking around the travel office, I could see beautiful pictures of the countryside, including Machu Picchu. Gosh, how I wished this were a vacation to explore beyond just a transit to some rock deep in the Peruvian mountains. On the other side, when I released the DNA virus, a portion of the tourists would breathe into their lungs the element of change that would unleash a plague of death across this planet.

"William, this time of year the trains are normally full, but the tourist volume has decreased substantially with the recent world chaos. Many people have either cancelled their holiday or headed home. There are plenty of options for you to consider for tomorrow."

"That sounds great and the earlier, the better," I said.

"Well, I think the Peru Rail out of Poroy leaving at 7:42 AM would be a good bet for you."

"Is Poroy here in Cusco?" I asked.

"No, Poroy station is about 30 minutes northwest of Cusco. Most people just catch a taxi to get to the station," stated Elicia.

"That sounds fine. Now, once I catch the train to Poroy, what is next on the trip to Machu Picchu?"

"The train will arrive in Agua Calientes around 10:51 AM, and that should provide you plenty of time to catch the bus that will take you to Machu Picchu, or if you feel hearty, you can take the trail hike."

Well, that sounded easy enough for a trail hike or bus ride, but I had better keep things low key and not convey any additional plans to Elicia.

"Elicia, that sounds great. I think when I get to Aqua Callientes I can decide on the hike or bus," I said coolly with a smile.

"Yes, many tourists from Europe go for the hike up to Machu Picchu for enjoyment and beauty."

Considering my level of hiking and endurance was stunted as a professor, I wasn't sure if the hike would work for me. My couch potato lifestyle didn't do much for my overall health and well-being. In addition, the altitude might be more than I realized, and even now, I was feeling a little lightheaded and felt a headache coming on.

"The total price will be 250 sol, including my agency fee. I will just need your passport, and then I can issue the ticket."

Now comes the tough part, I'm going to have to pay off Elicia to issue me a ticket without any identification. Here it goes. I reached down into my money stash, pulled out 2000 sol, folded the bills in half, and said quietly, "Elicia, I hope this covers the transaction without my passport, which I have lost recently."

Elicia slowly unfolded the bills, looked me straight in the eye, and said, "William, this puts me in a very difficult position. Maybe we can do something to help you and put you down as a local resident."

I nodded my head and said, "That would be appreciated."

"But since this is a little risky for me and my agency, I may need a little bit more to cover this transaction," said Elicia, who seemed to be a resourceful person.

Rather than ask how much more, I decided to pull out another 2000 sol and hope she would go for it. I again folded the bills in half and slid them slowly across her desk to her awaiting hands. Elicia pulled the bills under the desk then looked at me and said, "All appears in order. When will you be returning?" said Elicia as she smiled at me.

I provided midafternoon to Elicia as my return time for the following day, and she continued typing away on the computer with who knows what information to cover the transaction. She provided a fake local last name for issuing the ticket. Gosh, I'm sure glad the place was small and discreet. If all went well, I wouldn't trigger some global alarm on my whereabouts. I just needed to stay calm and not allow my nervousness to show.

"All right, I have printed out the departure and return tickets. Please look them over and let me know if all is okay."

Looking over the tickets, they both looked official, and the times and dates were correct. "Yes, all looks in order for travel," I said with a smile.

"Is there anything else I can do for you?"

"Well, since I have to stay one night here in Cusco, do you have any recommendations? Maybe a place that doesn't ask for my passport?" I said with a flat smile.

"Well, I have a good friend who runs a hostel, mostly for young people. That may work. How does that sound?" Elicia asked.

"Sounds like a great idea."

"Okay, give me a minute, and I will make a call to confirm she has a spot. Again, this is a peak time of the year, but there are fewer tourists with the world in turmoil," said Elicia with a sad look on her face, presumably considering that her business would be dismal this season.

"Yes, the world has for sure gone a bit crazy in the last several weeks," I said in response. Crazy…what would it be like in another few weeks? More like somewhere over the rainbow as the entire human population was reset. A hostel, now that will also be a new one for me since I have only stayed at hotels in the past. If all worked out, a good night's sleep and I would be out of here tomorrow morning.

"William, I spoke to my associate, and she has a hostel room available tonight. It's just a short walk from here, and when you get to the counter, just mention my name. The owner, Melissa, is from the UK, and she will take care of accommodations for you."

"That sounds great. Thank you for all the arrangements," I said, grabbing my tickets and exiting the travel agency. I was glad that was over; my stomach was churning over the effort it took to provide a bribe over a passport.

I needed to get a quick bite, find this hostel, and settle down for the night. Walking along and only viewing this world from the Discovery Channel made being here unimaginable. The high mountain fresh air and occasional food smells from the restaurant were a treat compared to my former sterile world in Idaho. When the time came for the release of the DNA virus, who knew how this world might rise back to life and the second coming of the Inca Empire. What an interesting world that would be as people banded together to learn the ancient methods all over again. Moving huge rocks and building incredible temples not be toppled by another civilization that brings greed, gold fever, and diseases that wipe out the indigenous populations.

Walking the streets, the multi-colored stucco buildings, trinket shops, and local costumes added to the flavor of this place that I didn't expect after just a few days of meandering through a tropical jungle filled with unknown trepidation. I could get used to this place and hopefully in a few days can wander back here to live out the consequences of my actions. Let's see if the small map of Elicia works for me to arrive at the Hostel with little effort.

"Señor, tal vez algunos jewlery para su esposa," said a friendly-looking woman in Spanish.

I waved my hand towards her, not having any idea what she had just said and provided a smile with a quick no thank you. She was persistent as I walked away and waved a few Inca dolls that were not on my consideration for today. I decided at this point that it was best to accept the Inca doll. I provided her with 50 sol and walked away, knowing money might be meaningless in a few weeks.

Ahhh. There it is Mama Simona Hostel. It looked quaint enough for one night. Walking up to the counter, I saw a young man who must have been expecting me since he perked up and said, "Welcome to Mama Simona."

"Thanks, I was referred to this place by Elicia from Cusco Travel Agency," I said, testing the waters.

"Yes, she called us and said to expect you."

"Great and I assume you have a room for me?"

"Yes, I have a private room for 80 sol if that works for you."

"Perfect, works for me," I said, hoping it was that easy to get a hostel room. I had no idea what to expect, but the word private sounded desirable and implied no communal accommodations.

"That will be 80 sol, and may I see your passport?" asked the young man.

Crud, not the elusive passport situation. Elicia must have tipped him off. How much to bribe this guy, who looked like he was living out a bohemian lifestyle as far as possible from his parents? Maybe 500 sol and that should at least keep him focused on checking me in.

I reached into my pocket and counted out 500 sol within sight of the young man so he could at least get an idea of what I was up to and said, "I think this should cover the room, and is there really a need for the passport?"

One of his eyebrows went up as he took the cash and said, "Thank you, enjoy your stay."

Thank God, this was easier than I thought and left me with as little guilt as could be expected for this type of transaction. As he handed me the key, he provided me with a piece of paper written in Spanish and English on the general rules of the hostel. "Your room is just around the corner, and if you need anything else, just let me know."

"Thank you. I appreciate your hospitality," I said, walking away. Now I needed to settle in, relax a bit, and just lay low. Whatever was in the backpack was going to have to serve as a quick lunch then maybe a quick dash for some food for dinner after it got dark. Keeping my guard up must be my first priority, even though everything from departing Colombia to arriving here had been flawless. When in doubt, expecting the worst and preparing for an exit strategy was always in Helen's priority. I would need to ask the hostel guy how to catch a taxi around six to ensure making the train the next morning at 7:42 AM. I didn't want to be late or miss it for any reason since this was my only chance to finish the mission.

The next morning…

"Liam, Liam…we have to go. We can't take a rest or there's the possibility of being tracked. I know you're tired, but the world is waiting for us to create the change that will save the planet. I won't let you down," said the voice of Helen, waking me up!

Whoa, was that Helen speaking to me or just a set of thoughts coming out of my head? I really missed having her next to me and sharing her life and wisdom. What a mind she had and an amazing personality of love, life, and empathy to save the human population that she was willing to sacrifice her life for us. Whew, waking up from such a dream I really feel lonely right now and alone on this mission.

It was 5:00 AM and not too early to get dressed and have a quick breakfast from the backpack and get rolling again. The travel agency woman mentioned 30 minutes, but I should consider hitting the road by 6:00 AM in order to provide a safety margin. Who knows what to expect: rain, a landslide, or the taxi breaking down? I was sure the first trains out of the station were always on time and didn't wait for stragglers for departure.

A quick wash-up – my beard was looking healthy these days to add to my elusive disguise. Though it could use a scissor or trimmer touch-up, it didn't matter right now. Heck, this might be the norm in a few weeks when the supply of razor blades dried up and people scavenged for the last remnants. I guess the population can live unshaven with respect to the primary consideration of survival. Vanity taking a back seat was probably going to be good overall for the humans. Whoa, I was starting to think like Helen about my fellow humankind.

I headed down to the front office, and an attendant was already busy getting ready for the day ahead by sweeping the floor.

"Good morning," I said.

"Bueno dias," said the attendant.

"Sorry, I don't speak any Spanish," I said, hoping for English from this woman.

"Not a problem. I speak some English."

"I'm just checking out and all paid up. I just need help to get a taxi," I said.

"No problem. What time would be good for you?"

"Well, now would be fine, and I need to get to Poroy train station," I said, assuming she knew the location since I was sure it was a very popular place.

"Give me a few minutes, and I will call one of my friends. He should be able to take you," the attendant said with a friendly smile.

"Gracias," I said.

Cool all set. I would taxi over to the station, jump on the train, and then be one-step closer to the final destination, which was starting to weigh heavily on my mind. I needed to run through my head the sequence of pushing the rock bumps that would release the DNA virus. It sounded simple enough but was still a long way off after a train trip to Machu Picchu Mountains. I wondered what went through Noah's head as he shut the doors to the boat, realizing the end was near with each drop of rain and that the people would die around him as the boat drifted away. I was sure it was a burden he would bear for the rest of his life despite the change it would bring to the world as a cataclysmic reset of the planet. I didn't want to be Noah or even remembered as he was. I just wanted to get the job done and walk away. Only me, my conscience, and the future of the people left behind was my concern. If I died in a few weeks, maybe it would be the best for myself and everyone else.

"Señor, the taxi will be here in five minutes. Since it's a little early, I would suggest a nice tip for the driver. He is a very nice man and has many niños to care for."

"Thank you for arranging it," I said and handed her 100 sol, which brought a smile to her face. Having plenty of money, I needed to unselfishly give it away. Heck, I still had the bag of diamonds available.

"Hola Taxi?" asked an older man as he walked through the door.

"Yes, I'm waiting for the taxi," I said in response as the man acknowledged my presence.

"Yo no hablo inglés," he said.

I looked over to the hostel attendant, and she immediately stepped in to help me out, which was great. I could hear the words Poroy, gringo, and mucho sol mentioned all in the same sentence. My mental translation was that the white guy needs to get to Poroy station, and he has lots of money to tip.

Okay, whatever it took from here forward; greasing the path with cash worked for me. Off to catch the train and just ease my mind the journey is coming to an end.

Waiting for the train…

I arrived with plenty of time ahead of the train departure, and observing the boarding process, it looked like all they were asking for was a ticket. That should make it much easier than having to slip some cash to the train attendant. The ticketed seat I got appeared to be on the trailing end of the train in the economy section. I had no problem since the trip was only around four hours, and that would give me time to catch a quick nap. Every sight along the way would only be a memory since I had no camera or phone to take pictures with like most of the tourists waiting for the train. Looking in their faces, I could see their excitement at heading to Machu Picchu. A few kids were in tow, but mostly mid to later ages of people were congregating around the terminal departure point. These were possibly the future carriers of the virus that was to be released. Helen had stated that a small percentage of the human race would be left after the virus spread across the world. With no cure, the most likely scenario she said was that the first wave would be gone within two weeks and the rest over several months. I didn't want to think about it anymore.

"Hello, mister, are you going to Machu Picchu?" said a youngster who appeared to be around eight years old.

"Yes, I'm going. How about you?" I said, smiling at him and his parents nearby.

"Are you all by yourself?" asked the young kid.

Hmmm, that was unexpected. All around me were couples or families getting ready to board the train. Yes, it would have been great to have a companion along with me on this trip and of course even better if it had been Helen. We could cuddle up in the seats sort of, like we did on the bus ride in Mexico. I can still remember that moment fondly being next to more or less a stranger but with a close connection already building.

"Yes, I'm by myself. My close friend wasn't able to make it," I said.

"Oh, well, hope to see you on the top."

"Likewise, and enjoy your trip," I said as his parents motioned him back to their side.

Departure time was announced, so it was off on the final stretch of the mission. It was best I stayed near the back and tried to blend in as the bohemian, disheveled traveler. Passing my ticket to the attendant wasn't a problem, and he smiled and thanked me as I moved over to the train car. The train looked very well kept, and seats two abreast with a center aisle looks appropriate. I expected there would be many empty seats even though this time of year was usually the peak season. World chaos and turmoil had halted the travel of all but the hardiest and adventure minded. Statistically, for the airborne virus to spread it needed just a very small portion of the travelers to get on planes or public transportation around the globe; then the virus would do the rest.

My seat had a window, which was nice for a four-hour trip to Aguas Calientes. It should be great. It looked like this train cabin was quite sparsely populated, with most people upgrading to the finer cabins up front. Considering how much I paid, including the under the table donation, I should have the train conductor's seat. Since only my backpack was with me, I stuffed it under the unoccupied seat next to me.

The train wheels were moving forward, hearing the metal-to-metal contact as they slid past each other. The exterior view of the town was similar to the taxi ride, with an assortment of homes under repair or in turmoil due to the weather conditions. It sort of felt like traveling through the small towns of Mexico. Various states of wealth, poverty, and divisions among the population.

A man and woman sitting on the opposite aisle appeared very content but worn out, as if they had traveled a long way to get here. I smiled to acknowledge their presence but let them be. There was no reason to disturb a couple on vacation. It was best to just get comfortable, close my eyes, and sleep or relax for the next several hours.

The explosion…

The sudden impact was unimaginable as I flew and toppled in my seat with a quick look out the window as chaos ensued. I could hear screams throughout the train along with windows breaking, metal being torn, and smoke billowing ahead. As the shaking and tumbling halted, by some miracle, the train car was upright, but outside the broken window, I could see the front section of the cars toppled and people who had been thrown aside. A portion of the front section of the train was scattered in the river. My section was spared, to my relief looking at other fellow disheveled passengers.

Looking around, I saw my pack sitting in the aisle just ahead of me; best to pick it up and get out of here before anything else transpires. I was sure the police, medical personnel would be here shortly, and slipping away undetected might be best. The couple that was next to me appeared slightly injured along with a few other people. However, it was not the time or place to help them. I need to leave now!

Was this explosion meant for me? Would bad people take out an entire train to get to me? Yes, they would. Now I needed to consider that someone was most likely watching for that one stranger to slip away. With my beard and scruffy look, they may have lost me in the shuffle, but I needed to

consider how to bug out of here undetected. Ahh…
there were a few people who looked as if someone
was directing them to town, so I could join them. I
assumed it was best to get the uninjured out of the
way so people could triage the critically injured that
could be saved. I didn't even want to look in the
direction where a portion of the train went into the
river. It was obvious people were dead.

"Sir, are you okay?" asked what looked like one of
the train personnel as I passed by.

"Yes, I'm fine to walk to town," I said, considering
my body felt a little beat up from the tumble in the
train. I should be able to make it the short walk to
the town with no problem. From there, I had to
figure out how to make my move up the mountain
to Machu Picchu. Joining at least thirty people,
I started my walk away from the disaster over the
secondary bridge crossing the river. I could see
the mobilization of people coming out to help the
wounded approaching from the town. There was a
small, hidden alley, where I could duck out of the
group and leave the chaos of the disaster.

It looked like a small market ahead, and
there should be some local people I could ask
about how to get up the mountain without being
noticed. Surviving without a high speed Internet
in this situation was more difficult than I would
imagine. If in Idaho, I would have found an answer
in thirty seconds, but here, I needed to depend on
local information.

"Hola, Señor habla Inglés?" I asked a merchant selling sweaters and other trinkets.

"Si, but just a little," he said with a motion of his fingers for small.

"I'm going to Machu Picchu but I lost my guide. What is the best way to reach the mountain?" I asked with a smile to build on my story as a lost foreigner.

"Si, there are only two ways. One is a bus and not expensive, and there is also a walking trail that will take you around one and a half hours," said the man.

"Great. I think the trail sounds possible. Can you point me in the right direction?"

"You will need to hike the Carretera Hiram Bingham trail. If you follow Avenida Hermanos Ayar Street, it will dead end right into the trail," said the man as he pointed to the sign showing the street name and what direction to proceed in.

"Gracias" I said and handed him 100 sol in gratitude. He in turn raised his eyebrows in appreciation.

All right…99% of the way to the final point in this mission. Helen, please watch over me because I have a feeling this is going to be the most difficult part of the trip. In a few hours, pending no additional tragic factors, the end would come. I knew in my heart that the reset of the world was in my hands. This one human out of the billions would light the flame to change the world.

On the trail...

Whoa, this hike wasn't quite what I expected, and the altitude must be the reason for the splitting headache. That was the last thing I needed, and even hydrating wasn't helping. The beauty of this place was magnificent, and the Incas had a mindset for the monumental in building this outpost high in the Andes. I could only imagine people moving rocks, scraping dirt, and planning these amazing feats of architecture. Then the coordination of bringing all the skills and knowledge to move huge rocks around and on top of each other was overwhelming. An incredible civilization was brought down by greed for land and gold by others. In addition, the diseases killed the majority of the population, which had no resistance to the foreign incursion. Then again, if I think forward, not much has changed, and look at where we are today on the verge of governments collapsing, economic chaos, and people detonating nuclear weapons to bring civilization to its knees.

"Whoa, sorry, I didn't see you there," I said, looking into a woman's eyes as she sat on a rock.

"No problem. Between the hike and switchbacks, it gets overwhelming," she said.

"Are you doing okay?" I asked.

"Truthfully, not so good, and I know this is most likely only the halfway point."

She didn't appear very well with her face pale, and I could see that her clothes were worn and dirty.

Something wasn't right, since I would expect foreign travelers to be in much better shape and looking more prepared for the trail.

Best to introduce myself and see how that goes. "My name is William," I said as I moved forward to shake her hand. I decided it was better to stick with William since I never knew whom to trust. As I reached forward to shake her hand, it was very sweaty and hot, as if she was running a fever or something.

"Nice to meet you. My name is Nahid," she said with a foreign accent. I couldn't determine the country of origin.

"That is a very pretty name. May I ask where you are from?"

"I grew up in the Middle East and have traveled far from home."

"Well, you sort of have that archeologist look rather than your normal tourist," I said, hoping to elicit a response to gain more insight.

"I guess you can call me a visitor with a mission," Nahid said.

Mission…mission…she said that with a serious look as if Helen was eliciting the response.

"Nahid, I don't mean to be inconsiderate, but you don't look well," I said with concern. She looked down at the ground with an expression of being troubled.

"William, I don't know you, and I have no idea if I can trust you," she said with a weak voice.

"Well, I can't disagree with you, but I'm not sure how I can help you."

Slowly, Nahid pulled back her jacket, and I could see that her left side was soaking in blood. Whoa, this was the last thing I expected.

"Oh my, you are badly hurt," I said with utmost confusion.

"Yes, I took a bullet that ripped through my side, but I don't think it hit anything vital," Nahid said.

"Okay enough, I don't need a story; let's get to work fixing you up. I have somewhat of a first aid kit and some painkillers that should at least help you out."

Cleaning up the wound was not what I expected to face on this final portion of the trip up the mountain. It appeared that the bullet passed through her soft side muscle, and I was sure the pain was intense. After blotting up the blood, I pulled out some ointment and smeared it on and into the wound, which resulted in piercing pain for Nahid as she bit her tongue. I applied the dressing then wrapped a bandage around her small torso. She provided a thankful smile, but her condition really required a medical doctor.

"I have some Ibuprofen to ease the pain," I said.

"That would be great," Nahid said as she accepted the pills and quickly proceeded to down them with water.

"The Ibuprofen will take a little while to kick in, and then you can head back," I said with a hint of immediate need. There was no way this girl should be on this trail.

"I can't. I must finish what I started out to do, and failure isn't acceptable!" exclaimed Nahid with a stern voice.

"Seriously, you need to go down. How about you wait here, and when I return, I can help you down the trail," I said.

"William, I'm not one to ask for assistance, but I need your help," Nahid said, reaching out to touch my hand. Her touch brought back memories of that first time when Helen did the same. What should I do with Nahid? She could slow me down or be a plant to stop me.

"Nahid, how about we hide your pack, and I can help you the best I can up to the top? That is the best I can offer you," I said with sincerity.

Looking with appreciation Nahid said, "Deal and thank you so much for your kindness."

As Nahid got up, I could see it was a struggle, but she appeared to be one tough cookie. My logical mind was starting to think—why was she here, why was she so determined to make it to the top, and why at this exact moment in time did I run into this woman? It was way too weird and something was starting to feel a little Helen like in this scenario. Maybe I could test her resolve.

"Nahid, how are you doing?" I asked while steadying her gait.

"Not bad, William, but we have to make the final push quickly before I fade."

"Yes, no problem. We will get you to the top for your mission," I said, looking her straight in the eye.

The comment caught her off guard as she looked at me with a way too quick motion. Let's see what

I could say next to gain a bit more insight into this mystery woman.

"So tomorrow the world will change," I said.

Looking at me with some level of annoyance, Nahid responded, "What exactly do you mean by the world will change?"

"Something you're planning on doing," I said.

Suddenly, Nahid turned around and pushed me enough to catch my foot on a rock, and I hit the ground. That must have got her attention! She quickly moved to place her foot directly on my chest, and she meant business no doubt.

"Okay, William, who in the hell are you?" Nahid asked with a very stern voice.

"Take your foot off my chest, and maybe we can talk," I said.

"No, talk now."

"Well, when you said mission, that meant something to me," I said.

"Okay, go on," said Nahid.

"You are heading up the mountain for a reason, and I just have a strange feeling we are somehow aligned for a reason," I said with a small glint of a smile.

"Well, if we were aligned, I don't need to be with you. I just need your help to get me to the top, and then we part ways, period," Nahid said sternly.

Looking at Nahid convinced me she was somehow connected, but her guard was 100% up to protect something. Was she just a secret agent or the real thing and carrying the same mission as I was?

"Okay, okay…no more questions. Let's continue," I said.

Nahid removed her foot off my chest and reached with a hand to help me off the ground, although she winced when my weight affected her injured side. It was best just to focus on getting her to the top while keeping a very close eye on her since she didn't trust me any more than I trusted her.

"Hey, sorry to be rough on you." said Nahid with a small hint of compassion.

That was most likely the only apology I would get out of Nahid. "Not a problem. Let's get moving."

The remaining portion of the hike up to the top was more than difficult for Nahid as we stopped at every switchback to allow her a recovery period. Exchange of words were few as I focused on not falling myself and providing her support. The pain medicine I provided to her must have been doing the trick because I could tell that her words were becoming less stressed. Though her English was good, it still carried the home country accent that challenged my attention. I had many foreign students from all over the world, so I had learned to speak slower and steady to ensure comprehension.

"William, we are near the top and will be parting ways," said Nahid.

"Yes, I understand, but how will you get off the mountain?" I asked, hoping to gain a greater understanding of this woman.

"William, I don't think it will really matter if I make it off this mountain. I have come so very far to this point, and by the will of my maker, I shall bear my soul to what I have to do," Nahid said as she looked down and around, as if her life was on a short string. Should I take the chance to connect with her? No, it was probably not a good idea to go any further with her. I would just drop her off at the top and carry on with my own mission.

"Well, Nahid, it looks like we have reached the point where our paths must part," I said.

"Yes, William this is where we have to say goodbye," Nahid said as she reached over to give me a hug that came as a surprise.

"I hope all the best for you," I said with a small smile.

"You too, my friend," Nahid said as she moved off into the distance.

CHAPTER 21 ♈ THE MEEK SHALL INHERIT THE EARTH

The time had come to take the final few steps in this journey. Somehow, by the grace of God, I had been spared to reach this point. Why me out of the billions of people on this planet? Mister no name philosophy professor from Moscow, Idaho, was standing on this mountain of the ancient past that would ensure the future evolution of humankind. My thoughts sounded monumental but not in consideration of the turmoil I would be unleashing on the world. Helen spoke of the uncertainty of the survival rate and, for that matter, if I would be part of the living. The survival population left behind with the empathy trait to push humankind forward. If her words were true, then billions to millions of people would be left to pick up the pieces as survivors of this world. I wasn't sure if I would be part of the rebirth of the world considering that right now I was lost in my own ethical emotions. All I had to do was find the five bumps on some stonewall and push them in the sequence provided by Helen. It was simple enough, and then I could sit back and hope something happened. This galactic civilization couldn't have made it much easier for a lone human to act. Push buttons, step back, and allow things to unfold.

I needed to get my head back in the game, walking past the entrance and paying was at least painless, with no need to bribe anyone. The place before my eyes wasn't of this world; the stones and architecture were more than my eyes could take in. I wished time could turn backwards for a moment and my life could take this in just as an awesome vacation—being able to take photographs to show my friends, climbing over these gigantic boulders, and having a grand adventure. Nevertheless, the voice in my head continued to speak to me: "Liam, this is your time." I knew it was Helen edging me on to the final steps in this long trek to this beautiful place that was like the gates to heaven.

The map brochure showed the sacred plaza, principal temple, temple Del Condor, Santuario Sagrado de Machu Picchu, and other places. Where in the world would these galactic types hide five bumps on a wall for me to push?

"Excuse me," said what appeared to be a park attendant.

"Yes?" I said.

"Are you lost, or do you need any help?" she asked.

"Well, actually, I'm sort of hoping to interpret some of these names on the map."

"Let me help you," she said politely.

Little did the woman know she could be assisting me by proxy on the future plight of the human race. At least she spoke good English; that made it easy to converse with her.

"Yes, can you give me an idea what these names mean in English," I said as I pointed to the various locations.

"Sure, let's see…Temple of the Condor, Sacred Sanctuary of Machu Picchu, Home of the Nobles, Temple of the Sun, and Temple of the Three Widows." She continued as I thought about her words. Where would the rock bumps be that aligned to the mission? Gosh, it would be nice to have Helen by my side; she would most likely find the exact spot without question. Maybe I just needed to sit on those rock steps, close my eyes, and just dream about my past before I ended the world.

"Thank you for your assistance," I said waving as the park attendant moved along.

Sitting down, I could feel the cool mountain air blow across my face; the scenery here was amazing, but it still held a taste of the last holdout for the great Inca Empire as it was brought to its knees by a handful of European conquers with diseases that eventually killed a huge portion of the population. In a way, it was somewhat ironic for me to be here and on the same sort of mission, where the DNA virus would spread through the worldly population unhindered.

Shutting my eyes, I felt my mind begin to drift; the touch that Helen had provided now came back to me, and my thoughts began to wander. I could see a garden in the far-off distance with people tending the plants and children playing with their pets. The sun was out, and a few clouds drifting by as the springtime brought a sense of prosperity. Simple homes could be viewed in the background, with a few trees to shade the homes and chimneys slowly spewing smoke into the air. My mind drifted further, as if something was embedded in the light…an expansive city lay calmly before my eyes. I couldn't view any cars or chaotic traffic crawling around the city. It was as if there was no need for such things or such forms of transportation. People were walking around, and riding their bikes, and some type of train system was elevated in various spots. In the background, a set of buildings that appeared to be far advanced above anything that would be characteristic of the present. Was this the future I was seeing? Did Helen plant something inside my head to encourage me to take the final push forward? She had touched me many times, and I always felt something special had penetrated my mind, but it was nothing like this. Was this the last thing she had given me as she lay dying—a pulse of humankind's future?

There she stood before me…Helen…Helen… as I looked out across a broad expanse of grass in an open meadow. She was beautiful, with a look of peace and a small smile that I knew was for me. "Liam, look for the Sanctuary," I heard inside my mind, "The Sanctuary."

Whoa…as I opened my eyes, what transpired was unreal. It was as if a video had unwound in my head and I was provided a timely message. This was the last message from Helen, no doubt, giving me the guidance to find the Sanctuary. The attendant had mentioned the Machu Picchu Sanctuary, and that was where I needed to be. Looking down at the map, I should be able to find it down this dirt path. It was time to head in that direction and look for the five bumps.

Walking along, I saw people wandering around who looked like they had arrived from many different countries. They would be the seeds to spread the virus, if all went well. Just a few microbes in their lungs and the airborne disease would incubate, and in a few weeks, it would spread around the planet before any symptoms could be detected.

Approaching the Sanctuary location, I noted there were many people congregating—and then before me was Nahid. She sat there looking straight ahead at a wall with five bumps. Why Nahid was sitting there was a mystery. Was she waiting to finish me off, or was she expecting me?

"Hello," I said to Nahid as I approached. I could tell she remained in pain as she held her side and looked up at me.

"William, I thought I would never see you again," she said with a look of surprise.

I needed to make a leap of faith; maybe she was here for the same reason. Could she be the mirror of me, traveling across the planet to reach this point?

"So did you enter the code?" I said without hesitation.

As Nahid looked up at me, there was a connection I didn't expect, and she said, "Yes, I did, and nothing happened. Or if it did, it passed right by me unnoticed."

"I believe we are both here for the same reason. Are you from the galactic society or human?" I asked.

"I'm just a normal human being on a quest placed before me by my host, who didn't make it," she said.

Whoa…this couldn't be possible.

"I'm essentially in the same position as you, brought to this place after traveling a tortuous path that resulted in the death of a very special person," I said with all apprehension of trusting her gone. Nahid was here just like me and for the same reason.

"So you put in the code, touched all the stone bumps, and nothing happened?" I asked.

"Yep, nothing after traveling all this fricking way, losing my own friend, getting shot and nothing," Nahid said with a long sigh of grief.

Think, Liam…something is wrong…or maybe it's right. Here sat before my eyes a carbon copy of an individual who started somewhere else on the planet and had come to this exact spot. However, she was a woman. What was that telling me? It had to mean something. One man, one woman traveling to this spot on the planet to release a DNA virus, yet nothing happened—or maybe that was what was supposed to happen.

"Nahid, what was the code you used?" I asked. She looked at me, and I could feel a sense of mistrust since for all she knew, I could be her death sentence—a pursuer out to get the final code and stop her.

"How do I know if I can trust you? I have come this far, but I'm not sure if you are my end," Nahid said with a stiff upper lip.

"I tell you what. I'm going to turn my back to you. You reach forward and put in your code, and I won't be able to see it. Then once you are done, I will do the same. If I'm right, the activation takes one man and one woman with possibly different codes as a failsafe. In that case, you and I both needed to make it this far."

"I never thought of that, but that makes a lot of sense. I agree," Nahid said.

I turned my back, wishing I knew what code Nahid was entering. After a few seconds, she tapped me on the shoulder, and said, "Not sure who should have gone first, but it's your turn."

As Nahid turned her back to me, I looked around for the last time. This was my moment. I reached out and touched the bumps, just as Helen had instructed.

'The activation sequence is from right to left. Touch each individually for one to two seconds. Once that is done, quickly push the center three bumps from left to right just once, step back and the mission is done.'

As I pushed the last bump, a small electrostatic shock went straight up my arm and into my head!

The rumble started as I turned to Nahid, and her eyes widened as the huge rock split open with a cataclysmic crack that echoed through our heads and a vibration that felt like an earthquake shuddering from the bowels of the earth. Looking up into the air, a cloud of mist rose hundreds of feet and quickly radiated into the air with a light smell of lilacs.

A crowd of people came forward to see what was going on with a huge rock that had just split open. I was sure they thought the mist was just rock dust, but I knew otherwise since the light scent was the message that our mission was done.

"We may have had different codes or maybe the same, but it took both of us together. I think our mission is complete!" exclaimed Nahid.

"Yes, I think we were brought together to finish the mission, and somehow the future of humankind rested on both of our shoulders to work together. One man, one woman—to make the final decision that would change the world and evolve humankind."

"Are you all right?" asked Nahid with deep empathy in her voice.

"Yes, I think I'm all right," I said, considering my far-off life in Idaho was gone forever.

As I stood there silently looking at the people wandering over to view the split rock, the mist settled on all of us. Would I survive the virus? Truthfully, it really didn't matter. This was the right thing to do.

While standing side by side with Nahid, she reached over gently to hold my hand and gave it a light squeeze. I knew this wasn't the end as I felt the warmth of her touch reach deep into my soul.

THE END...FOR THE BEGINNING

EPILOGUE

As an eccentric author, I hope you enjoyed this story and it promotes a little empathy in your heart for others on this planet...if you have it! ☺

Ψ (Psi)
What Is an Empath—and Can You Become One?
"According to a study on empathy, published in Nature Neuroscience, only one to two percent of the population consists of true empaths."
Charlotte Hilton Andersen - January 2021
www.thehealthy.com/mental-health/what-is-an-empath
Ψ (Psi)
The Decline of Empathy And The Rise Of Narcissism

"Like most things in psychology, there's lots of research showing that empathy has a genetic component, about half of empathy that a baby is born with is a genetic component"

Sara Konrath, PhD - December 2019 www.apa.org/research/action/speaking-of-psychology/empathy-narcissism

Ψ (Psi)

What Is Empathy, And Can Empathy Be Taught?

"The act of empathizing cannot be taught. According to Edith Stein, a German phenomenologist, empathy can be facilitated. It also can be interrupted and blocked, but it cannot be forced to occur."

"What makes empathy unique, according to Stein, is that it happens to us; it is indirectly given to us, "non primordially." When empathy occurs, we find ourselves experiencing it, rather than directly causing it to happen"

C M Davis - November 1990

https://pubmed.ncbi.nlm.nih.gov/2236214/